40p

Michael Moorcock is astonishing. His enormous output includes around fifty novels, innumerable short stories and a rock album. Born in London in 1939, he became editor of *Tarzan Adventures* at sixteen, moving on later to edit the *Sexton Blake Library*. He has earned his living as a writer/editor ever since, and is without doubt one of Britain's most popular and most prolific authors. He has been compared with Tennyson, Tolkien, Raymond Chandler, Wyndham Lewis, Ronald Firbank, Mervyn Peake, Edgar Allan Poe, Colin Wilson, Anatole France, William Burroughs, Edgar Rice Burroughs, Charles Dickens, James Joyce, Vladimir Nabokov, Jorge Luis Borges, Joyce Cary, Ray Bradbury, H. G. Wells, George Bernard Shaw and Hieronymus Bosch, among others.

'No one at the moment in England is doing more to break down the artificial divisions that have grown up in novel writing – realism, surrealism, science fiction, historical fiction, social satire, the poetic novel – than Michael Moorcock.'
Angus Wilson

'He is an ingenious and energetic experimenter, restlessly original, brimming over with clever ideas.'
Robert Nye, *The Guardian.*

D0320367

Also by Michael Moorcock

The Cornelius Chronicles
The Final Programme
A Cure for Cancer
The English Assassin
The Condition of Muzak
The Lives and Times of Jerry Cornelius
The Adventures of Una Persson and Catherine Cornelius in the Twentieth Century

The Dancers at the End of Time
The Hollow Lands
An Alien Heat
The End of All Songs
Legends from the End of Time
The Transformation of Miss Mavis Ming (Return of the Fireclown)

Hawkmoon: The History of the Runestaff
The Jewel in the Skull
The Mad God's Amulet
The Sword of the Dawn
The Runestaff

Hawkmoon: The Chronicles of Castle Brass
Count Brass
*The Champion of Garathorm**
*The Quest for Tanelorn**

Erekosë
The Eternal Champion
Phoenix in Obsidian
*The Champion of Garathorm**
*The Quest for Tanelorn**

Elric Series
Elric of Melniboné

The Sailor on the Seas of Fate
The Sleeping Sorceress
The Stealer of Souls
Stormbringer
Elric at the End of Time

The Books of Corum
The Knight of the Swords
The Queen of the Swords
The King of the Swords
The Bull and the Spear
The Oak and the Ram
The Sword and the Stallion

Other titles
The City of the Beast
The Lord of the Spiders
The Masters of the Pit
The Warlord of the Air
The Land Leviathan
The Winds of Limbo
Behold the Man
Breakfast in the Ruins
The Blood-Red Game
The Black Corridor
The Chinese Agent
The Distant Suns
The Rituals of Infinity
The Shores of Death
Sojan the Swordsman (juvenile)
The Golden Barge
Gloriana (or, *The Unfulfill'd Queene, a Romance*)
The Time Dweller (short stories)
Moorcock's Book of Martyrs (short stories)
Heroic Dreams (non-fiction)
Entropy Tango
    * interconnected series

Michael Moorcock

The Bull and the Spear

Volume the First of
*The Chronicle of Prince Corum
and the Silver Hand*

MAYFLOWER
GRANADA PUBLISHING
London Toronto Sydney New York

Published by Granada Publishing Limited
in Mayflower Books 1979

ISBN 0 583 12984 6

First published by Allison & Busby Ltd 1973
Copyright © Michael Moorcock 1973

Granada Publishing Limited
Frogmore, St Albans, Herts AL2 2NF
and
3 Upper James Street, London W1R 4BP
866 United Nations Plaza, New York, NY 10017, USA
117 York Street, Sydney, NSW 2000, Australia
100 Skyway Avenue, Rexdale, Ontario, M9W 3A6, Canada
PO Box 84165, Greenside, 2034 Johannesburg, South Africa
CML Centre, Queen and Wyndham, Auckland 1, New Zealand

Made and printed in Great Britain by
Hunt Barnard Printing Ltd, Aylesbury, Bucks
Set in Monotype Garamond

This book is sold subject to the condition that it
shall not, by way of trade or otherwise be lent,
re-sold, hired out or otherwise circulated
without the publisher's prior consent in any
form of binding or cover other than that in
which it is published and without a similar
condition including this condition being imposed
on the subsequent purchaser.

Granada ®
Granada Publishing ®

For Marianne

PROLOGUE

In those days there were oceans of light and cities in the skies and wild flying beasts of bronze. There were herds of crimson cattle that roared and were taller than castles. There were shrill, viridian things that haunted bleak rivers. It was a time of gods, manifesting themselves upon our world in all her aspects; a time of giants who walked on water; of mindless sprites and misshapen creatures who could be summoned by an ill-considered thought but driven away only on pain of some fearful sacrifice; of magics, phantasms, unstable nature, impossible events, insane paradoxes, dreams come true, dreams gone awry; of nightmares assuming reality.

It was a rich time and a dark time. The time of the Sword Rulers. The time when the Vadhagh and the Nhadragh, age-old enemies, were dying. The time when Man, the slave of fear, was emerging, unaware that much of the terror he experienced was the result of nothing else but the fact that he, himself, had come into existence. It was one of many ironies connected with Man (who, in those days, called his race Mabden).

The Mabden lived brief lives and bred prodigiously. Within a few centuries they rose to dominate the westerly continent on which they had evolved. Superstition stopped them from sending many of their ships toward Vadhagh and Nhadragh lands for another century or two, but gradually they gained courage when no resistance was offered. They began to feel jealous of the older races; they began to feel malicious.

The Vadhagh and the Nhadragh were not aware of this. They had dwelt a million or more years upon the planet which now, at last, seemed at rest. They knew of the Mabden, but considered them not greatly different from other beasts. Though continuing to indulge their traditional hatreds of one another, the Vadhagh and the Nhadragh spent their long hours in considering abstractions, in the creation of works of art and the like. Rational, sophisticated, at one with themselves, these older races were unable to believe in the changes that had come. Thus, as it almost always is, they ignored the signs.

There was no exchange of knowledge between the two ancient enemies, even though they had fought their last battle many centuries before.

The Vadhagh lived in family groups occupying isolated castles scattered across a continent called by them Bro-an-Vadhagh. There was scarcely any communication between these families, for the Vadhagh had long since lost the impulse to travel. The Nhadragh lived in their cities built on the islands in the seas to the northwest of Bro-an-Vadhagh. They, also, had little contact, even with their closest kin. Both races reckoned themselves invulnerable. Both were wrong.

Upstart Man was beginning to breed and spread like a pestilence across the world. This pestilence struck down the old races wherever it touched them. And it was not only death that Man brought, but terror, too. Wilfully, he made of the older world nothing but ruins and bones. Unwittingly, he brought psychic and supernatural disruption of a magnitude which even the Great Old Gods failed to comprehend.

And the Great Old Gods began to know fear.

And Man, slave of fear, arrogant in his ignorance, continued his stumbling progress. He was blind to the huge disruptions aroused by his apparently petty ambitions. As well, Man was deficient in sensitivity, had no awareness of the

2

multitude of dimensions that filled the universe, each plane intersecting with several others. Not so the Vadhagh or the Nhadragh, who had known what it was to move at will between the dimensions they termed the Five Planes. They had glimpsed and understood the nature of many planes, other than the Five, through which the Earth moved.

Therefore it seemed a dreadful injustice that these wise races should perish at the hands of creatures who were still little more than animals. It was as if vultures feasted on and squabbled over the paralysed body of the youthful poet who could only stare at them with puzzled eyes as they slowly robbed him of an exquisite existence they would never appreciate, never know they were taking.

'If they valued what they stole, if they knew what they were destroying,' says the old Vadhagh in the story 'The Only Autumn Flower', 'then I would be consoled.'

It was unjust.

By creating Man, the universe had betrayed the old races. But it was a perpetual and familiar injustice. The sentient may perceive and love the universe, but the universe cannot perceive and love the sentient. The universe sees no distinction between the multitude of creatures and elements which comprise it. All are equal. None is favoured. The universe, equipped with nothing but the materials and the power of creation, continues to create: something of this, something of that. It cannot control what it creates and it cannot, it seems, be controlled by its creations (though a few might deceive themselves otherwise). Those who curse the workings of the universe curse that which is deaf. Those who strike out at those workings fight that which is inviolate. Those who shake their fists, shake their fists at blind stars.

But this does not mean that there are not some who will try to do battle with and destroy the invulnerable.

There will always be such beings, sometimes beings of great wisdom, who cannot bear to believe in an insouciant universe.

Prince Corum Jhaelen Irsei was one of these. Perhaps the

last of the Vadhagh race, he was sometimes known as the Prince in the Scarlet Robe.

This is the second chronicle, concerning his adventures. The first chronicle, known as 'The Books of Corum', told how the Mabden followers of Earl Glandyth-a-Krae killed Prince Corum's relatives and his nearest kin and thus taught the Prince in the Scarlet Robe how to hate, how to kill, and how to desire vengeance. We have heard how Earl Glandyth tortured Prince Corum and took away a hand and an eye and how Corum was rescued by the Giant of Laahr and taken to the castle of the Margravine Rhalina – a castle set upon a mount surrounded by the sea. Though Rhalina was a Mabden woman (of the gentler folk of Lwym-an-Esh), Corum and she fell in love. When Glandyth roused the Pony Tribes, the forest barbarians, to attack the Margravine's castle, she and Corum sought supernatural aid and thus fell into the hands of the sorcerer Shool, whose domain was the island called Svi-an-Fanla-Brool–Home of the Gorged God. And now Corum had direct experience of the morbid, unfamiliar powers at work in the world. Shool spoke of dreams and realities ('I see you are beginning to argue in Mabden terms,' he told Corum. 'It is just as well for you, if you wish to survive in this Mabden dream.' – 'It is a dream . . . ?' said Corum. – 'Of sorts. Real enough. It is what you might call the dream of a God. Then again you might say that it is a dream that a God has allowed to become reality. I refer of course to the Knight of the Swords, who rules the Five Planes . . .').

With Rhalina his prisoner, Shool could make a bargain with Corum. He gave him two gifts – the Hand of Kwll and the Eye of Rhynn – to replace his own missing organs. These jewelled and alien things were once the property of two brother gods known as the Lost Gods since they mysteriously vanished.

Armed with these Corum began his great quest, which was to take him against all three Sword Rulers – the Knight, the Queen and the King of the Swords – the mighty Lords of Chaos. And Corum discovered much concerning these gods, the nature of reality and the nature of his own identity. He learned that he was the Champion Eternal, that, in a thousand

4

other guises, in a thousand other ages, it was his lot to struggle against those forces which attacked reason, logic and justice, no matter what form they took. And, at long last, he was able to overwhelm (with the help of a mysterious ally) those forces and banish gods from his world.

Peace came to Bro-an-Vadhagh and Corum took his mortal bride to his ancient castle which stood on a cliff overlooking a bay. And meanwhile the few surviving Vadhagh and Nhadragh turned again to their own devices, and the golden land of Lwym-an-Esh flourished and became the centre of the Mabden world – famous for its scholars, its bards, its artists, its builders and its warriors. A great age dawned for the Mabden folk; they flourished. And Corum was pleased that his wife's folk flourished. On the few occasions when Mabden travellers passed near Castle Erorn he would feast them well and be filled with gladness when he heard of the beauties of Halwyg-nan-Vake, capital city of Lwym-an-Esh, whose walls bloomed with flowers all year round. And the travellers would tell Corum and Rhalina of the new ships which brought great prosperity to the land, so that none in Lwym-an-Esh knew hunger. They would tell of the new laws which gave all a voice in the affairs of that country. And Corum listened and was proud of Rhalina's race.

To one such traveller he offered an opinion: 'When the last of the Vadhagh and the Nhadragh have disappeared from this world,' he said, 'the Mabden will emerge as a greater race than ever were we.'

'But we shall never have your powers of sorcery,' answered the traveller, and he caused Corum to laugh heartily.

'We had no sorcery at all! We had no conception of it. Our "sorcery" was merely our observation and manipulation of certain natural laws, as well as our perception of other planes of the multiverse, which we have now all but lost. It is the Mabden who imagine such things as sorcery – who would always rather invent the miraculous than investigate the ordinary (and find the miraculous therein). Such imaginations will make your race the most exceptional this Earth has yet known, but those imaginations could also destroy you!'

'Did we invent the Sword Rulers whom you so heroically fought?'

'Aye,' answered Corum, 'I suspect that you did! And I suspect that you might invent others again.'

'Invent phantoms? Fabulous beasts? Powerful gods? Whole cosmologies?' said the astonished traveller. 'Are all these things, then, unreal?'

'They're real enough,' Corum replied. 'Reality, after all, is the easiest thing in the world to create. It is partly a question of need, partly a question of time, partly a question of circumstance . . .'

Corum had felt sorry for confounding his guest and he laughed again and passed on to other topics.

And so the years went by and Rhalina began to show signs of age while Corum, near-immortal, showed none. Yet still they loved each other – perhaps with greater intensity as they realised that the day drew near when death would part her from him.

Their life was sweet; their love was strong. They needed little but each other's company.

And then she died.

And Corum mourned for her. He mourned without the sadness which mortals have (which is, in part, sadness for themselves and fear of their own death).

Some seventy years had passed since the Sword Rulers fell, and the travellers grew fewer and fewer as Corum of the Vadhagh people became more of a legend in Lwym-an-Esh than he was remembered as a creature of ordinary flesh. He had been amused when he had heard that in some country parts of that land there were now shrines to him and crude images of him to which folk prayed as they had prayed to their gods. It had not taken them long to find new gods and it was ironic that they should make one of the person who had helped rid them of their old ones. They magnified his feats and, in so doing, simplified him as an individual. They attributed magical powers to him; they told stories of him which they had once told of their previous gods. Why was the truth never enough for the Mabden? Why must they forever embellish and obscure

6

it? What a paradoxical people they were!

Corum recalled his parting with his friend, Jhary-a-Conel, self-styled Companion to Champions, and the last words he had spoken to him – 'New gods can always be created,' he had said. Yet he had never guessed, then, from what at least one of those gods would be created.

And, because he had become divine to so many, the people of Lwym-an-Esh took to avoiding the headland on which stood ancient Castle Erorn, for they knew that gods had no time to listen to the silly talk of mortals.

Thus Corum grew lonelier still; he became reluctant to travel in Mabden lands, for this attitude of the folk made him uncomfortable.

In Lwym-an-Esh those who had known him well, known that, save for his longer lifespan, he was as vulnerable as themselves, were now all dead, too. So there were none to deny the legends.

And, likewise, because he had grown used to Mabden ways and Mabden people about him, he found that he could not find much pleasure in the company of his own race, for they retained their remoteness, their inability to understand their situation, and would continue to do so until the Vadhagh race perished for good. Corum envied them their lack of concern, for, though he took no part in the affairs of the world, he still felt involved enough to speculate about the possible destiny of the various races.

A kind of chess, which the Vadhagh played, took up much of his time (he played against himself, using the pieces like arguments, testing one strain of logic against another). Brooding upon his various past conflicts, he doubted, sometimes, if they had ever taken place at all. He wondered if the portals to the fifteen planes were closed forever now, even to the Vadhagh and the Nhadragh, who had once moved in and out of them so freely. If this were so, did it mean that, effectively, those other planes no longer existed? And thus his dangers, his fears, his discoveries, slowly took on the quality of little more than abstractions; they became factors in an argument concerning the nature of time and identity and, after a while,

7

the argument itself ceased to interest Corum.

Some eighty years were to pass since the fall of the Sword Rulers before Corum's interest was to be re-awakened in matters concerning the Mabden folk and their gods.

THE CHRONICLE OF CORUM AND THE SILVER HAND

Book One

In which Prince Corum finds himself dreaming an unlikely and unwelcome dream . . .

1. FEARING THE FUTURE AS THE PAST GROWS DIM

Rhalina, ninety-six years old, and handsome, had died, Corum had wept for her. Now, seven years later, he still missed her and he contemplated his own lifespan of perhaps another thousand years and envied the race of Mabden its brief years, yet shunned the company of that race, because he was reminded of her.

Dwelling again in their isolated castles – whose forms so mirrored the natural rock that many Mabden passing by could not see them for buildings at all but mistook them for outcrops of granite, limestone and basalt – were his own race, the Vadhagh. These he shunned because he had grown, while Rhalina lived, to prefer Mabden company. It was an irony about which he would write poetry, or paint pictures, or compose music in the several halls of Castle Erorn set aside for the purpose.

And thus he grew strange, in Castle Erorn by the sea.

He grew remote. His retainers (all Vadhagh now) wondered how to express to him their view that perhaps he should take a Vadhagh wife, by whom he might have children and through whom he might discover a renewed interest in the present and the future. But there was no way they could find to approach their lord, Corum Jhaelen Irsei, Prince of the Scarlet Robe, who had helped conquer the most powerful gods and rid this world of much that it had feared.

The retainers began to know fear. They grew to fear Corum, that lonely figure, with an eye-patch covering an empty socket, with his variety of artificial right hands, each one of exquisite craftsmanship (made by Corum for his own use), that silent strider in midnight halls, that moody rider through the winter woods.

And Corum knew fear, too. He felt a fear of empty days, of lonely years, waiting through the slow-turning centuries for death.

He contemplated ending his life, but somehow he felt that such an action would be an insult to Rhalina's memory. He considered embarking upon a quest, but there were no lands to explore in this bland, this warm, this tranquil world. Even the bestial Mabden of King Lyr-a-Brode had returned to their original pursuits, becoming farmers, merchants, fishermen, miners. No enemies threatened, no injustice was evident. Freed from gods, the Mabden had become content, kindly and wise.

Corum recalled the old pursuits of his youth. He had hunted. But now he had lost any relish he had ever had for the chase. He had been hunted too frequently during his battle with the Sword Rulers to feel anything now but anguish for the pursued. He had ridden. He had relished the lush and lovely countryside landward of Castle Erorn. But his relish for life had waned. He still rode, however.

He would ride through the broadleaf forests which skirted the promontory on which Castle Erorn was raised. Sometimes he would venture as far as the deep, green moor beyond with its thick gorse, its hawks, its skies and its silence. Sometimes he would take the coast road back to Castle Erorn, riding dangerously close to the crumbling cliff edge. Far below, the high, white surf would rear against the rocks, hissing and growling. Sometimes tendrils of spray would strike Corum's face, but he would hardly feel them. Once such sensations had made him grin with pleasure.

On most days Corum would not venture out. Neither sun, nor wind, nor rattling rain would lure him from the gloomy rooms which had, in the days when his family occupied them and, later, when Rhalina occupied them, been replete with love and light and laughter. Sometimes he would not move, even, from his chair. His tall, slender body would sprawl upon the cushions, he would rest his beautiful, tapering head upon his fleshly fist and his almond-shaped yellow and purple eye would stare into the past, a past which grew dimmer all the time and increased his desperation as he strove to remember every detail of his life with Rhalina. A prince of the great Vadhagh folk, grieving for a mortal woman. There had never been ghosts in Castle Erorn before the Mabden came.

And sometimes, when he did not yearn for Rhalina, he would wish that Jhary-a-Conel had not decided to leave this plane, for Jhary, like him, was apparently immortal. The self-styled Companion to Heroes seemed able to move at will through all the fifteen planes of existence, acting as a guide, a foil, a counsellor to one whom, in Jhary's opinion, was Corum in several different guises. It had been Jhary-a-Conel who had said that he and Corum could be 'aspects of a greater hero', just as, in the tower of Voilodion Ghagnasdiak, he had met two other aspects of that hero, Erekosë and Elric. Jhary had claimed that those two were Corum in other incarnations and it was Erekosë's particular doom to be aware of most of those incarnations. Intellectually, Corum could accept such an idea, but emotionally he rejected it. He was Corum. And that was his doom.

Corum had a collection of Jhary's paintings (most of them self-portraits, but some were of Rhalina and of Corum and of the small black and white winged cat which Jhary took everywhere with him, as he took his hat). Corum, in his most morbid moments, would study the portraits, recalling the old days, but slowly even the portraits came to be those of strangers. He would make efforts to consider the future, to make plans regarding his own destiny, but all his intentions came to nothing. There was no plan, no matter how detailed, how reasonable, which lasted more than a day or so. Castle Erorn was littered with unfinished poems, unfinished prose, unfinished music, unfinished painting. The world had turned a man of peace into a warrior and then left him with nothing to fight. That was Corum's fate. He had no reason to work the land, for Vadhagh food was grown within the castle walls. There was no shortage of meat or wine. Castle Erorn provided all its few inhabitants needed. Corum had spent many years working on a variety of artificial hands, based on what he had seen at the doctor's house in the world of Lady Jane Pentallyon. Now he had a selection of hands, all perfect, which worked as well for him as any hand of flesh had done. His favourite, which he wore most of the time, was one which resembled a finely-wrought gauntlet in filigreed silver, an exact match to the hand which Earl Glandyth-a-Krae had cut off nearly a century before. This was the hand he could have used to hold his sword or his lance or his bow, had there been any call for him to use his weapons now. Tiny movements of the muscles in the stump of his original wrist would make it do everything an ordinary hand could do, and more, for the grip was stronger. Secondly, he had become ambidextrous, able to use his left hand as well as he had used his right hand. Yet all his skill could not make him a new eye and he had to be content with a simple patch, covered in scarlet silk and worked with Rhalina's fine needle into an intricate pattern. It was his unconscious habit, now, to run the fingers of his left hand frequently over the needlework as he sat brooding in his chair.

Corum began to realise that his taciturnity was turning to madness when, in his bed at night, he began to hear voices. They were distant voices, a chanting chorus which called a name which might be his in a language which resembled the Vadhagh tongue and yet which was unlike it. Try as he might, he could not drive the voices out, just as he could not, however much he strained his ears to listen, understand more than a few words of what they said. After several nights of these voices, he began to shout for them to stop. He would groan. He would roll in his silks and his furs and try to stuff his ears. And in the days he would try to laugh at himself, would go for long rides to tire himself so that he would sleep heavily. Yet still the voices would come to him. And, later, there were dreams. Shadowy figures stood in a grove in a thick wood. Their hands were linked in a circle, apparently surrounding him. In his dreams he would speak to them, saying that he could not hear them, that he did not know what they wanted. He asked them to stop. But they continued to chant. Their eyes were closed, their heads were flung back. They swayed.

'Corum. Corum. Corum. Corum.'

'What do you want?'

'Corum. Help us. Corum.'

He would break through their circle and run into the forest and then he would awake. He knew what had happened to him. His mind had turned in on itself. Not properly occupied it had begun to invent phantoms. He had never heard of such a thing happening to a Vadhagh, though it happened frequently enough to Mabden people. Did he, as Shool had once told him, still live in a Mabden dream? Was the dream of the Vadhagh and the Nhadragh completely over? And did he therefore dream one dream within another?

But these thoughts did not help his sanity. He tried to drive them away. He began to feel the need for advice, yet there was none to advise him. The Lords of Law and Chaos no longer ruled here, no longer had servants here to whom they imparted at least some of their knowledge. Corum knew more of philosophical matters than did anyone else. Yet there were wise Vadhagh who had come here from Gwlãs-cor-Gwrys, the City in the Pyramid, who knew something of these matters.

He determined that, if the dreams and the voices continued, then he would set off on a journey to one of the other castles where the Vadhagh lived and there seek help. At least, he reasoned, there was a good chance that the voices would not follow him from Castle Erorn.

His rides grew wilder and he tired all his horses. He went farther and farther away from Castle Erorn, as if he hoped to find something. But he found nothing but the sea to his west and the moors and the forests to his east, south and north. No Mabden villages were here, no farms or even the huts of charcoal-burners or foresters, for the Mabden had no desire to settle in Vadhagh lands, not since the fall of King Lyr-a-Brode. And was that really what he sought? Corum wondered. Mabden company? Did his voices and his dreams represent his desire to share adventures with mortals again? The thought was painful to him. He saw Rhalina clearly for a moment, as she had been in her youth, radiant, proud and strong.

With his sword he slashed at the stems of ferns. With his lance he drove at the boles of trees. With his bow he shot at rocks. A parody of battle. Sometimes he would fall upon the grass and sob.

And still the voices called him:

'Corum! Corum! Help us!'

'Help you?' he screamed back. 'It is Corum who needs help!'

'Corum. Corum. Corum...'

Had he ever heard those voices before? Been in a situation like this one before?

It seemed to Corum that he had, yet, as he recalled all the events in his life, he knew that it could not be true. He had never heard those voices, dreamed those dreams. And still he was sure that he remembered them from another time. Perhaps from another incarnation? Was he truly the Champion Eternal?

Weary, sometimes ragged, sometimes without his weapons, sometimes leading a limping horse, Corum would return to Castle Erorn by the sea and the pounding of the waves in the caves below Erorn would be like the pounding of his own heart.

His servants would try to comfort him, to restrain him, to ask him what ailed him. He would not reply. He was civil, but he would tell them nothing of his torment. He had no way of telling them and he knew that they would not understand, even if he could find a way.

And then, one day, as he stumbled across the threshold of the castle courtyard, barely able to keep himself from falling, the servants told him that a visitor had come to Castle Erorn and that he waited for Corum in one of the music chambers which Corum had had closed for some years, for the sweetness of the music had reminded him too much of Rhalina, whose favourite chamber it had been.

'His name?' Corum muttered. 'Is he Mabden or Vadhagh? His purpose here?'

'He would tell us nothing, master, save that he was either your friend or your enemy—that you would know that.'

'Friend or enemy? A riddler? An entertainer? He'll have hard work here. . . .'

Yet Corum was curious, almost grateful for the mystery. Before he went to the music room he washed himself and put on fresh clothes and drank a little wine until he felt revived enough to face the stranger.

The harps and the organs and the crystals in the music chamber had begun their symphony. He heard the faint notes of a familiar tune drifting up to his apartments. At once he felt overwhelmed by depression and determined that he would not do the stranger the courtesy of receiving him. But something in Corum wanted to listen to that music. He had composed it himself, one year, for Rhalina's birthday. It expressed much of the tenderness he had felt towards her. She had then been ninety years old, with her mind and body as sound as they had ever been. 'You keep me young, Corum,' she had said.

Tears came into Corum's single eye. He brushed them away, cursing the visitor who had revived such memories. The man was a boor, coming uninvited to Castle Erorn, opening up a deliberately closed chamber. How could he justify such actions?

And then Corum wondered if this were a Nhadragh, for the Nhadragh, he had heard, still hated him. Those who had remained alive after King Lyr-a-Brode's conquests had degenerated into semi-sentience. Had one of them remembered just enough of his hatred to seek out Corum to slay him? Corum felt something close to elation at this thought. He would relish a fight.

And so he strapped on his silver hand and his slender sword before he went down the ramp to the music chamber.

As he neared the chamber the music grew louder and louder, more complex and more exquisite. Corum had to struggle against it as he might struggle against a strong wind.

He entered the room. Its colours swirled and danced with

17

the music. It was so bright that Corum was momentarily blinded. Blinking, he peered around the chamber, seeking his visitor.

Corum saw the man at last. He was sitting in the shadows, absorbed in the music. Corum went amongst the huge harps, the organs and the crystals touching them and quieting them until, at last, there was complete silence. The colours faded from the room. The man rose from his corner and began to approach. He was small of stature and walked with a distinct swagger. He had a wide-brimmed hat upon his head and a deformity on his right shoulder, perhaps a hump. His face was entirely obscured by the brim of the hat, yet Corum began to suspect that he knew the man.

Corum recognised the cat first. It sat upon the man's shoulder. It was what Corum had at first mistaken for a hump. Its round eyes stared at him. It purred. The man's head lifted and there was the smiling face of Jhary-a-Conel.

So astonished was Corum, so used was he to living with ghosts, that at first he did not respond.

'Jhary?'

'Good morrow, Prince Corum. I hope you did not mind me listening to your music. I don't believe I have heard that piece before.'

'No. I wrote it long after you left.' Even to his own ears, Corum's voice was distant.

'I upset you, playing it?' Jhary became concerned.

'Yes. But you were not to blame. I wrote it for Rhalina and now . . .'

'Rhalina is dead. I heard she lived a good life. A happy life.'

'Aye. And a short life.' Corum's tone was bitter.

'Longer than most mortals', Corum.' Jhary changed the subject. 'You do not look well. Have you been ill?'

'In my head, perhaps. I still mourn for Rhalina, Jhary-a-Conel. I still grieve for her, you see. I wish she . . .' Corum offered Jhary a somewhat bleak smile. 'But I must not consider the impossible.'

'Are there impossibilities?' Jhary gave his attention to his cat, stroking its fur-covered wings.

'There are in this world.'

'There are in most. Yet what is impossible in one is possible in another. That is the pleasure one has in travelling between the worlds, as I do.'

'You went to seek gods. Did you find them?'

'A few. And some heroes whom I could accompany. I have seen a new world born and an old one destroyed, since we last talked. I have seen many strange forms of life and heard many peculiar opinions regarding the nature of the universe and its inhabitants. Life comes and goes, you know. There is no tragedy in death, Corum.'

'There is a tragedy here,' Corum pointed out. 'When one has to live for centuries before rejoining the object of one's love – and then only joining her in oblivion.'

'This is morbid, silly talk. It is unworthy of a hero.' Jhary laughed. 'It is unintelligent, to say the least, my friend. Come now, Corum – I'll regret paying you this visit if you've become as dull as that.'

And at last Corum smiled. 'You are right. It is what happens to men who avoid the company of their fellows, I fear. Their wits grow stale.'

'It is for that reason that I have always, by and large, preferred the life of the city,' Jhary told him.

'Does the city not rob you of your spirit? The Nhadragh lived in cities and they grew degenerate.'

'The spirit can be nurtured almost anywhere. The mind needs stimuli. It is a question of finding the balance. It also depends upon one's temperament, too, I suppose. Well, temperamentally I am a dweller in cities. The larger, the dirtier, the more densely populated, the better! And I have seen some cities so black with grime, so packed with life, so vast, that you would not believe me if I told you the details! Ah, beautiful!'

Corum laughed. 'I am pleased that you have come back, Jhary-a-Conel, with your hat and your cat and your irony!' And then they embraced each other and they laughed together.

2. THE INVOCATION OF A DEAD DEMIGOD

That night they feasted and Corum's heart lightened and he enjoyed his meat and wine for the first time in seven years.

'And then I came to be involved in the strangest of all adventures concerning the nature of time,' Jhary told him. Jhary had been recounting his deeds for nearly two hours. 'You'll recall the Runestaff, which came to our aid during the episode concerning the tower of Voilodion Ghagnasdiak? Well, my adventures touched on the world most influenced by that peculiar stick. A manifestation of that eternal hero, of whom you, yourself, are a manifestation, he called himself Hawkmoon. If you think that your tragedy is great, you would think it nothing when you heard the tragedy of Hawkmoon, who gained a friend and lost a bride, two children and . . . ' And for another hour he told the tale of Hawkmoon.

There were other tales to follow, he promised, if Corum wished to hear them. There were tales of Elric and Erekosë, whom Corum had met, of Kane and Cornelius and Carnelian, of Glogauer and Bastable and many more. All aspects, Jhary swore, of the same champion and all his friends (if not himself). And he spoke of such weighty matters with so much humour, with so many joking asides, that Corum's spirits rose still higher, until he was helpless with laughter and quite drunk on the wine.

Then, in the early morning, Corum confided to Jhary his secret – that he feared that he had gone mad.

'I hear voices, dream dreams – always the same. They call for me. They beg me to join them. Do I pretend to myself that this is Rhalina who calls me? Nothing I do will rid me of them, Jhary. That is why I was out again today – hoping to tire myself so much that I would not dream.'

And Jhary's face became serious as he listened. And when Corum had finished, the little man put a hand on his friend's shoulder, saying, 'Fear not. Perhaps you have been mad, these past seven years, but it was a quieter madness altogether. You did hear voices. And the people you saw in your dream were real people. They were summoning – or trying to summon – their champion. They were trying to bring you to them. They have been trying for many days now.'

Again Corum had difficulty in understanding Jhary. 'Their champion . . . ?' he said vaguely.

'In their age you are a legend,' Jhary told him. 'A demigod, at very least. You are Corum Llaw Ereint to them – Corum of the Silver Hand. A great warrior. A great champion of his people. There are whole cycles of tales concerning your exploits and proving your divinity!' Jhary smiled a little sardonically. 'As with most gods and heroes you have a legend attached to your name, which says that you will return at the time of your people's greatest need. Now their need is great indeed.'

'Who are these people that they should be "mine"?'

'They are the descendants of the folk of Lwym-an-Esh – Rhalina's people.'

'Rhalina's . . . ?'

'They are a fine folk, Corum. I know them.'

'You come from them now?'

'Not exactly.'

'You cannot make them stop this chanting? You cannot make them cease appearing in my dreams?'

'Their strength weakens daily. Soon they will trouble you no longer. You will sleep tranquilly again.'

'Are you sure?'

'Oh, I am certain. They can survive for only a little while more, before the Cold Folk overwhelm them. Before the People of the Pines enslave or slay what remains of their race.'

'Well,' said Corum, 'as you say, these things come and go. . . .'

'Aye,' said Jhary. 'But it will be sad to see the last of that golden folk go down beneath the dark and savage invaders who now sweep across their land, bringing terror where there was peace, bringing fear where there was joy. . . .'

'It sounds familiar,' said Corum dryly. 'So the world turns, and turns again.' He was now fairly well satisfied that he understood why Jhary was harping upon this particular subject.

'And turns again,' agreed Jhary.

'And even if I would, I could not help them, Jhary. I am no longer able to travel between the planes. I cannot even see through to other planes. Besides, how could one warrior help this folk of which you speak?'

'One warrior could help greatly. And it is their invocation which would bring you to them, if you would let it. But they are weak. They cannot summon you against your will. You resist them. It does not take much resistance. Their numbers grow small, their power fades. They were once a great people. Even their name derives from your name. They call themselves Tuha-na-Cremm Croich.'

'Cremm?'

'Or Corum, sometimes. It is an older form. It means simply "Lord" to them – Lord of the Mound. They worship you in the form of a stone slab erected on a mound. You are supposed to live beneath that mound and hear their prayers.'

'These are superstitious people.'

'A little. But they are not god-ridden. They worship Man above all else. And all their gods are really nothing more than dead heroes. Some folk make gods of the sun, the moon, the storms, of the beasts and so on. But this folk deifies only what is noble in Man and loves what is beautiful in nature. You would be proud of your wife's descendants, Corum.'

'Aye,' said Corum, narrowing his eye and giving Jhary a sideways look. There was a faint smile on his lips. 'Is this mound in a forest. An oak forest?'

'An oak forest, yes.'

'It is the same that I saw in my dream. And why is this folk attacked?'

'A race from beyond the sea (some say from beneath the sea) comes from the east. The whole land which used to be named Bro-an-Mabden has either gone under the waves or lies beneath a perpetual cloak of winter. Ice covers all – brought by this eastern folk. It has also been said that this is a folk that once conquered this land and was driven back. Others suggest that it is a mixture of two old races, or more, banded together to destroy the ancestors of the Mabden of Lwym-an-Esh. There is no talk of Law or Chaos there. If this folk has power, it comes from themselves. They can produce phantasms. Their spells are powerful. They can destroy either by means of fire or by means of ice. And they have other powers, too. They are called the Fhoi Myore and they control the North Wind. They are called the Cold Folk and they can make the northern and the eastern seas answer their bidding. They are called the People of the Pines and can command black wolves as their servants. They are a brutal people, born, some say, of Chaos and Old Night. Perhaps they are the last vestiges of Chaos upon this plane, Corum.'

Corum was smiling openly now. 'And you urge me to go against such a folk? On behalf of another folk which is not my own?'

'Your own by adoption. Your wife's folk.'

'I have already fought in one conflict that was not my own,' said Corum, turning away and pouring himself more wine.

'Not your own? All such conflicts are yours, Corum. It is your fate.'

'And what if I resist that fate?'

'You cannot resist it for any great time. I know that. It is better to accept your destiny with good grace – with humour, even.'

23

'Humour?' Corum swallowed the wine and wiped his lips. 'That is not easy, Jhary.'

'No. But it is what makes the whole thing bearable.'

'And what do I risk if I answer this call and help that folk?'

'Many things. Your life.'

'That is worth little. What else?'

'Your soul, perhaps.'

'And what is that?'

'You could discover the answer to that question if you embark upon this enterprise.'

Corum frowned. 'My spirit is not my own, Jhary-a-Conel. You have told me that.'

'I did not. Your spirit is your own. Perhaps your actions are dictated by other forces. Another question altogether. . . .'

Corum's frown changed as he smiled. 'You sound like one of those priests of Arkyn who used to thrive in Lwym-an-Esh. I think the morality is somewhat doubtful. However, I was ever pragmatic. The Vadhagh race is a pragmatic race.'

Jhary raised his eyebrows, but said nothing. 'Will you allow yourself to be called by the People of Cremm Croich?'

'I will consider it.'

'Speak to them, at least.'

'I have tried. They do not hear.'

'Perhaps they do. Or perhaps you must be in a certain frame of mind to answer so that they can hear.'

'Very well. I will try. And what if I do allow myself to be borne into this future time, Jhary? Will you be there?'

'Possibly.'

'You cannot be more certain?'

'I am not more master of my fate than are you, Champion Eternal.'

'I would be grateful,' said Corum, 'if you will not use that title. I find it discomforting.'

Jhary laughed. 'I cannot say that I blame you. Corum Jhaelen Irsei!'

Corum rose and stretched his arms. The firelight touched his silver hand and made it gleam red, as if suddenly suffused with blood. He looked at the hand, turning it this way and that in the light as if he had never properly seen it before. 'Corum of the Silver Hand,' he said musingly. 'They think the hand of supernatural origin, I take it.'

'They have more experience of the supernatural than what you would call "science". Do not despise them for that. Where they live there are strange things happening. Natural laws are sometimes the creation of human ideas.'

'I have often contemplated that theory, but how does one find evidence for it, Jhary?'

'Evidence, too, can be created. You are doubtless wise to encourage your own pragmatism. I believe everything, just as I believe nothing.'

Corum yawned and nodded. 'It is the best attitude to have, I think. Well, I'll to my bed. Whatever comes of all this, know that your coming has improved my spirits considerably, Jhary. I'll speak with you again in the morning. First I must see how this night passes.'

Jhary stroked his cat under its chin. 'You could benefit greatly from helping those who call to you.' It was almost as if he had addressed the cat.

Corum paused as he walked towards the door. 'You have already hinted as much. Can you tell me in what way I would benefit?'

'I said "could", Corum. I cannot say more. It would be foolish of me, and irresponsible. Perhaps it is already true that I have said too much. For now I puzzle you.'

'I'll dismiss the question from my mind – and bid you good night, old friend.'

'Good night, Corum, may your dreams be clear.'

Corum left the room and began to climb the ramp to his own bedchamber. This would be the first night in many months that he looked forward to sleep less with fear than with curiosity.

He fell asleep almost immediately. And, almost immediately, the voices began. Instead of resisting them, he relaxed and listened.

'Corum! Cremm Croich. Your people need you.'

For all its strange accent, the voice was quite clear. But Corum saw nothing of the chorus, nothing of the circle with linked hands which stood about a mound in an oak grove.

'Lord of the Mound. Lord of the Silver Hand. Only you can save us.'

And Corum found himself replying:

'How can I save you?'

The answering voice sounded excited. 'You answer at last! Come to us, Corum of the Silver Hand. Come to us, Prince in the Scarlet Robe. Save us as you have saved us in the past.'

'How can I save you?'

'You can find for us the Bull and the Spear and lead us against the Fhoi Myore. Show us how to fight them, for they do not fight as we fight.'

Corum stirred. Now he could see them. They were tall and good-looking young men and women whose bronzed bodies glinted with warm gold, the colour of autumn corn, and the gold was woven into intricate and pleasing designs. Armlets, anklets, collars and circlets, all of gold. Their flowing clothes were of linen dyed in light reds, blues and yellows. There were sandals upon their feet. They had fair hair or hair as red as rowan berries. They were, indeed, the same race as the folk of Lwym-an-Esh. They stood in the oak grove, hands joined, eyes closed, and they spoke as one.

'Come to us, Lord Corum. Come to us.'

'I will consider it,' said Corum, making his tone a kindly one, 'for it is long since I have fought and I have forgotten the arts of war.'

'Tomorrow?'

'If I come, I will come tomorrow.'

The scene faded, the voices faded. And Corum slept peacefully until morning.

When he awoke he knew that there was nothing to debate. While he slept he had decided, if possible, to answer the call of the people of the oak grove. His life at Castle Erorn was not only miserable, it served no one, not even himself. He would go to them, crossing the plane, moving through time, and he would go to them willingly, proudly.

Jhary found him in the armoury. He had selected for himself the silver byrnie and the conical helm of silvered steel with his full name engraved above the peak. He had found greaves of gilded brass and he had laid out his surcoat of scarlet silk, his shirt of blue samite. A long-hafted Vadhagh war-axe stood against a bench and beside it was a sword manufactured in a place other than the Earth, with a hilt of red and black onyx; a lance whose shaft was carved from top to bottom with miniature hunting scenes comprising more than a hundred tiny figures, all depicted in considerable detail; a good bow and a quiver of well-fletched arrows. Resting against these was a round war-board, a shield made of a number of layers of timber, leather, brass and silver and covered all over with the fine, strong hide of the white rhinoceros which had once lived in the northern forests of Corum's land.

'When do you go to them?' said Jhary, inspecting the array.

'Tonight.' Corum weighed the lance in his hand. 'If their summoning is successful. I shall go mounted, on my red horse. I shall ride to them.'

Jhary did not ask how Corum would reach them and Corum himself had not considered that problem, either. Certain peculiar laws would be involved and that was all they knew or cared to know. And much depended on the power of invocation of the group who waited in the oak grove.

Together, they broke their fast and then they went up to the battlements of the castle. From those battlements they could see the wide ocean to the west and the great forests and moors to the east. The sun was bright and the sky was wide and clear and blue. It was a good, peaceful day. They talked of the old times, recalling dead friends and dead or banished gods, of Kwll who had been more powerful than either the Lords of Law or the Lords of Chaos, who had seemed to fear nothing. They wondered where Kwll and his brother Rhynn had gone, whether there were other worlds beyond the fifteen planes of

Earth and if those worlds resembled Earth in any way.

'And then, of course,' said Jhary, 'there is the question concerning the Conjunction of the Million Spheres and what follows when that conjunction is over. Is it over yet, do you think?'

'New laws are established after the Conjunction. But established by what? And by whom?' Corum leaned against the battlements, looking out across the narrow bay. 'I suspect that it is we who make those laws. And yet we do so unknowingly. We are not even sure what is good and what is evil – or, indeed, if anything is either. Kwll had no such beliefs and I envied him. How pitiful we are. How pitiful am I that I cannot bear to live without loyalties. Is it strength which makes me decide to go to these people? Or is it weakness?'

'You speak of good and evil and say you know not what they are – it is the same with strength and weakness. The terms are meaningless.' Jhary shrugged. 'Love means something to me, and so does hate. Physical strength is given to some of us – I can see it. And some are physically weak. But why equate the elements in a man's character with such attributes. And, if we do not condemn a man because, through luck, he is not physically strong, why condemn him if, for instance, his resolve is not strong. Such instincts are the instincts of the beasts and, for beasts, they are satisfactory instincts. But men are not beasts. They are men. That is all.'

Corum's smile had some bitterness in it. 'And they are not gods, Jhary.'

'Not gods – or devils, either. Just men and women. How much happier would we be if we accepted that!' And Jhary threw back his head and laughed suddenly. 'But perhaps we should be more boring, too! We are both of us beginning to sound too pious, my friend. We are warriors, not holy men!'

Corum repeated a question of the previous night. 'You know this land, where I have decided to go. Shall you go there, too – tonight?'

'I am not my own master.' Jhary began to pace the flagstones.' 'You know that, Corum.'

'I hope that you do.'

'You have many manifestations in the fifteen planes, Corum. It could be that another Corum somewhere needs a companion and that I shall have to go with him.'

'But you are not sure?'

'I am not sure.'

Corum shrugged. 'If what you say is true – and I suppose I must accept that it is – then perhaps I shall meet another aspect of you, one who does not know his fate?'

'My memory often fails me, as I have told you before. Just as yours fails you in this incarnation.'

'I hope that we shall meet on this new plane and that we shall recognise one another.'

'That is my hope, also, Corum.'

They played chess that evening and spoke little and Corum went early to his bed.

When the voices came, he spoke to them slowly:

'I shall come in armour and I shall be armed. I shall ride upon a red horse. You must call me with all your powers. I give you time to rest now. Gather your strength and in two hours begin the invocation.'

In one hour Corum rose and went down to put his armour on, to dress himself in silk and samite, to have his ostler lead his horse into the courtyard. And when he was ready, with his reins in his gloved left hand and his silver hand upon the pommel of a poignard, he spoke to his retainers and told them that he rode upon a quest and that if he did not return they should throw open Castle Erorn to any traveller who needed shelter and that they should feast such travellers well, in Corum's name. Then he rode through the gates and down the slope and into the great wood, as he had ridden nearly a century before when his father and his mother and his sisters had been alive. But then he had ridden through the morning. Now he rode into the night, beneath the moon.

Of all those in Castle Erorn, only Jhary-a-Conel had not bid goodbye to Corum.

Now the voices grew louder in Corum's ears as he rode through the dark, ancient forest.

'Corum! Corum!'

Strangely, his body began to feel light. He touched spurs to the flanks of his horse and it broke into a gallop.

'Corum! Corum!'

'I am coming!' The stallion galloped harder, its hooves pounding the soft turf, plunging deeper and deeper into the dark wood.

'Corum!'

Corum leaned forward in his saddle, ducking as branches brushed his face.

'I come!'

He saw the shadowy group in the grove. They surrounded him, yet still he rode and his speed grew even faster. He began to feel dizzy.

'Corum!'

And it seemed to Corum that he had ridden like this before, that he had been called in this way before and that was why he had known what to do.

The trees blurred, he rode with such speed.

'Corum!'

White mist began to boil all round him. Now the faces of the chanting group could be seen in sharper detail. The voices grew faint, then loud, then faint again. Corum spurred the snorting horse on into the mist. That mist was history. It was legend. It was time. He glimpsed sights of buildings, the like of which he had never seen, rising hundreds and thousands of feet into the air. He saw armies of millions, he saw weapons of terrifying power. He saw flying machines and he saw dragons. He saw creatures of every shape, size and form. All seemed to cry out to him as he rode by.

And he saw Rhalina.

He saw Rhalina as a girl, as a boy, as a man, as an old woman. He saw her alive and he saw her dead.

And it was that sight which made him scream and it was why he was still screaming as he rode suddenly into a forest clearing, bursting through a circle of men and women who had stood with hands linked around a mound, and who chanted as with a single voice.

He was still screaming as he drew his bright sword and raised it high in his silver hand as he reined his horse to a halt on top of the mound.

'Corum!' cried the folk in the clearing.

And Corum ceased to scream and lowered his head, though his sword was still raised.

The red Vadhagh horse in all its silken trappings pawed at the grass of the mound and again it snorted.

Then Corum said in a deep, quiet voice. 'I am Corum and I will help you. But remember, in this land, in this age, I am a virgin.'

'Corum,' they said. 'Corum Llaw Ereint.' And they pointed out his silver hand to each other and their faces were joyful.

'I am Corum,' he said. 'You must tell me why I have been summoned.'

A man older than the others, his red beard veined with white, a great gold collar about his neck, stepped forward.

'Corum,' he said. 'We called you because you *are* Corum.'

3. THE TUHA-NA-CREMM CROICH

Corum's mind was clouded. For all that he could smell the night air, see the people around him, feel the horse beneath him, it still seemed that he dreamed. Slowly he rode back down the mound. A light wind caught the folds of his scarlet robe and lifted them, swirling them about his head. He tried to realise that somehow he was now separated from his own world by at least a millennium. Or could it be, he wondered, that he really did dream, still. He felt the detachment that he sometimes felt when he was dreaming. As he reached the bottom of the grassy mound the tall Mabden folk stood back respectfully. By the expressions on their well-formed features it seemed plain that they, too, were dazed by this event, as if they had not really expected their invocation to be successful. Corum felt sympathy with them. These were not the superstitious barbarians he had first suspected he would find. There was intelligence on those faces, a clarity about their gaze, a dignity about the way in which they held themselves, even though they thought they were in the presence of a supernatural being. These, it seemed, were the true descendants of the best of his wife's folk. At that moment he felt no regret that he had answered their summons.

He wondered if they felt the cold, as he did. The air was sharp and yet they wore only thin cloaks which left their arms, chests and legs bare, save for the gold ornaments, leather straps and high sandals which all, men and women, had.

The older man who had first spoken to Corum was powerfully built and as tall as the Vadhagh himself. Corum reined his horse before this man and he dismounted. They stared at each other for some moments. Then Corum spoke distantly:

'My head is empty,' he said. 'You must fill it.'

The man stared thoughtfully at the ground and then raised his head, saying:

'I am Mannach, a king.' He smiled faintly. 'A wizard, I, of sorts. Druid, some call me, though I've few of the Druids' skills—nor much of their wisdom. But I am the best we have now, for we have forgotten most of the old lore. Which is perhaps why we are now in this predicament.' He added, almost with embarrassment, 'We had no need of it, we thought, until the Fhoi Myore came back.' He looked curiously at Corum's face as if he disbelieved in the power of his own invocation.

Corum had decided almost at once that he liked this King Mannach. Corum approved of the man's scepticism (if that was what it was). Plainly the invocation had been weak because Mannach and probably the others had only half-believed in it.

'You summoned me when all else failed?' said Corum.

'Aye. The Fhoi Myore beat us in battle after battle, for they do not fight as we fight. At last we had nothing left but our legends.' Mannach hesitated and then admitted: 'I did not believe much in those legends before now.'

Corum smiled. 'Perhaps there was no truth in them before now.'

Mannach frowned. 'You speak more like a man than a god—or even a great hero. I mean no disrespect.'

'It is other folk who make gods and heroes of men like myself, my friend.' Corum looked at the rest of the gathering. 'You must tell me what you expect of me, for I have no mystic powers.'

It was Mannach who smiled now. 'Perhaps you had none before.'

Corum raised his silver hand. 'This? It is of earthly manufacture. With the right skills and knowledge any man might make one.'

'You have gifts,' said King Mannach. 'The gifts of your race, your experience, your wisdom – aye, and your skills, Lord of the Mound. The legends say that you fought mighty gods before the Dawn of the World.'

'I fought gods.'

'Well, we have great need of a fighter of gods. These Fhoi Myore are gods. They conquer our land. They steal our Holy things. They capture our people. Even now our High King is their prisoner. Our Great Places fall to them – Caer Llud and Craig Dôn among them. They divide our land and so separate our folk. Separated, it becomes harder for us to join in battle against the Fhoi Myore.'

'They must be numerous, these Fhoi Myore,' said Corum.

'There are seven.'

Corum said nothing, allowing the astonishment, which he had been unable to hide, to serve in place of words.

'Seven,' said King Mannach. 'Come with us now, Corum of the Mound, to our fort at Caer Mahlod, there to take meat and mead with us while we tell you why we called for you.'

And Corum remounted his horse and allowed the people to lead it through the frost-rimed oak wood and up a hill which overlooked the sea upon which a moon cast a leprous light. Stone walls rose high around the crown of the hill and there was only one small gate, really a tunnel which went down then up again, through which a visitor could pass in order to enter the city. These stones were white, too. It was as if the whole world were frozen and all its scenery carved from ice.

Within the city of Caer Mahlod reminded Corum of the stone cities of Lyr-a-Brode, though some attempts had been made to finish the granite of the houses' walls, to paint scenes upon the walls, to carve gables. Much more fortress than town, the place had a gloomy aspect Corum could not equate with the people who had summoned him.

'These are old forts,' King Mannach explained. 'We were driven from our great cities and forced to find homes here, where our ancestors were said to dwell. They are strong, at least, settlements like Caer Mahlod, and during the day it is possible to see many miles in all directions.' He ducked beneath a portal as he led Corum into one of the big buildings which was lit with rush torches and oil lamps. The others who had been with Mannach in the oak wood followed them in.

At last they all stood in a low-roofed hall furnished with heavy wooden benches and tables. On these tables, however, was some of the finest gold, silver and bronze plate Corum had ever seen. Each bowl, each platter, each cup, was exquisite and, if anything, of even finer workmanship than the ornaments the people wore. For all that the walls were of rough stone, the hall danced with glittering light as the flames of the brands were reflected in the tableware and the ornaments of the People of Cremm Croich.

'This is all that is left of our treasure," said King Mannach, and he shrugged. 'And the meat we serve is poor fare now, for game grows scarce, running before the Hounds of Kerenos which hunt the whole land as soon as the sun has set and do not cease hunting until the sun rises. One day, we fear, the sun will not rise again at all and soon the only life in all the world will be those hounds and the huntsmen who are their masters. And ice and snow will prevail over all – everlasting Samhain.'

Corum recognised this last word for it was like the word the folk of Lwym-an-Esh had used to describe the darkest and the bleakest days of winter. He understood King Mannach's meaning.

They seated themselves at the long wooden table and servants brought the meat. It was an unappetising meal and again King Mannach apologised for it. Yet there was little gloom in that hall this night as harpists played merry tunes and sang of the old glories of the Tuha-na-Cremm Croich and made up new songs describing how Corum Jhaelen Irsei would lead them against their enemies and destroy those enemies and bring back the summer to their land. Corum noticed with pleasure that men and women were on terms of complete equality here and he was told by King Mannach that the women fought beside the men in their battles, being particularly adept in the use of the battle-snare, the weighted thong which could be hurled through the air to encircle the throats of the enemy and strangle them or snap their necks or limbs.

'These are all things which we have had to learn again in the past few years,' Mannach told Corum, pouring him frothy mead into a large golden cup. 'The arts of battle had become little more than exercise, games of skill with which we entertained each other at festivals.'

'When did the Fhoi Myore come?' Corum asked.

'Some three years ago. We were unprepared. They arrived on the eastern shores during the winter and did not make their presence known. Then, when spring did not come in those parts, people began to investigate the causes. We did not believe it at first, when we heard what had happened from the folk of Caer Llud. Since then the Fhoi Myore have extended their rule until now the whole of the eastern half of this land, from top to bottom, has become their undisputed domain. Gradually they move westward. First come the Hounds of Kerenos, then come the Fhoi Myore.'

'The seven? Seven men?'

'Seven misshapen giants, two of which are female. And they have strange powers, controlling forces of nature, beasts and, perhaps, even demons.'

'They come from the east. Where in the east?'

'Some say from across the sea, from a great mysterious continent of which we know little, a continent now bereft of life and entirely covered in snow. Others say that they come from beneath the sea itself, from a land where only they can live. Both these lands were called by our ancestors Anwyn, but I do not think this is a Fhoi Myore name.'

'And Lwym-an-Esh? Do you know aught of that land?'

'It is where, in legend, our folk came from. But in ancient times, in the misty past, there was a battle between the Fhoi Myore and the folk of Lwym-an-Esh and Lwym-an-Esh was drawn beneath the sea to become part of the land of the Fhoi

Myore. Now only a few islands remain and on those islands are a few ruins, I have heard, speaking for the truth of the legends. After this disaster our people defeated the Fhoi Myore – with magical help in the form of a sword, a spear, a cauldron, a stallion, a ram and an oak tree. These things were kept at Caer Llud in the care of our High King, who had rule over all the different peoples of this land and who, once a year at midsummer, would mete out justice in any disputes thought to be too complicated for kings such as myself. But now our magical treasures are scattered – some say lost forever – and our High King is a slave of the Fhoi Myore. That is why, in desperation, we recalled the legend of Corum and begged you for your help.'

'You speak of mystical things,' said Corum, 'and I was never one to understand magics and the like, but I will try to help.'

'It is strange, what has happened to us,' mused King Mannach, 'for here I sit eating with a demigod, and discover that, in spite of the evidence of his own existence, he is as unconvinced by the supernatural as was I!' He shook his head. 'Well, Prince Corum of the Silver Hand, we must both learn to believe in the supernatural now. The Fhoi Myore have powers which prove that it exists.'

'And so have you, it seems,' added Corum. 'For I was brought here by an invocation distinctly magical in character!'

A tall red-haired warrior leaned across the table, raising a wine-cup high to toast Corum. 'Now we shall defeat the Fhoi Myore. Now their devil dogs shall run! Hail to Prince Corum!'

And all rose then, echoing the toast.

'Hail to Prince Corum!'

And Prince Corum acknowledged the toast and replied to it with:

'Hail to the Tuha-na-Cremm Croich!'

But in his heart he was disturbed. Where had he heard a similar toast? Not during his own life. Therefore he must recall another life, another time when he was hero and saviour to a people not unlike these in some ways. Why did he feel a

37

sense of dread, then? Had he betrayed them? Try as he might, he could not rid himself of these feelings.

A woman left her place on the bench and swayed a little as she approached him. She put a soft, strong arm about him and kissed his right cheek. 'Hail to thee, hero,' she murmured. 'Now you shall bring us back our bull. Now you shall lead us into battle with the spear Bryionak. Now you will restore to us our lost treasures and our Great Places. And will you sire us sons, Corum? Heroes?' And she kissed him again.

Corum smiled a bitter smile. 'I will do all else, if it is in my power, lady. But one thing, the last thing, I cannot do, for Vadhagh cannot sire Mabden children.'

She did not seem distressed. 'There is magic for that, too, I think,' she said. For the third time she kissed him before returning to her place. And Corum felt desire for her and this sense of desire reminded him of Rhalina and then he became sad again and his thoughts turned inward.

'Do we tire you?' King Mannach asked a little later.

Corum shrugged. 'I have been sleeping for too long, King Mannach. I have stored up my energy. I should not be tired.'

'Sleeping? Sleeping in the mound?'

'Perhaps,' answered Corum dreamily. 'I thought not, but perhaps it was in the mound. I lived in a castle overlooking the sea, wasting my days in regret and despair. And then you called. At first I would not listen, then an old friend came and told me to answer your call. So I came. But possibly that was the dream. . . .' Corum began to think he had quaffed too much of the sweet mead. It was strong. His vision was cloudy and he was filled with a peculiar mixture of melancholy and euphoria. 'Is it important to you, King Mannach, my place of origin?'

'No. What is important is that you are here at Caer Mahlod, that our people see you and take heart.'

'Tell me more of the Fhoi Myore and how you were defeated.'

'Of the Fhoi Myore I can tell you little, save that it is said they were not always united against us – that they are not all of the same blood. They do not make war as we once made war. It was our way to choose champions from the ranks of the contesting armies. Those champions would fight for us, man to man. matching skills until one was beaten. Then his life would be spared, if he had not sustained bad injuries from his fight. Often no weapons at all would be used – bard would match bard, composing satires against their enemies until the best satirist sent the others slinking away in shame. But the Fhoi Myore had no such notion of battle when they came against us. That is why we were defeated so easily. We are not killers, but that folk are killers. They want Death – crave for Death – follow Death – cry after Him to turn and face them. That folk, the Cold Folk, are like that. Those People of the Pines, they ride willy-nilly in pursuit of Death and herald the Reign of Death, of the Winter Lord, across all the land you ancients called Bro-an-Mabden, the Land in the West. This land. Now we have people in the north, the south and the west. Only in the east have we no people left, for they are cold now, fallen before the People of the Pines. . . .'

King Mannach's voice began to take on the aspects of a dirge, a lament for his people in their defeat. 'O Corum, do not judge us by what you see now. I know that we were once a great folk with many powers, but we became poor after our first fights with the Fhoi Myore, when they took away the land of Lwym-an-Esh and all our books and lore with it. . . .'

'This sounds like a legend to explain a natural disaster,' Corum said gently.

'So thought I until now,' King Mannach told him and Corum was bound to accept this.

'Though we are poor,' continued the king, 'and though much of our control over the inanimate world is lost, for all this, we are still the same folk. Our minds are the same. We do not lack intelligence, Prince Corum.'

Corum had not considered that they had. Indeed, he had been astonished at the king's clear thinking, having expected to meet a race much more primitive in its ideas. And though this people had come to accept magic and wizardry as a fact, they were not otherwise superstitious.

'Yours is a proud and noble people, King Mannach,' he said sincerely. 'And I will serve them as best I can. But it is

39

for you to tell me how to serve, for I have less knowledge of the Fhoi Myore than have you.'

'The Fhoi Myore have great fear of our old magical treasures,' King Mannach said. 'To us they had become little more than objects of interesting antiquity, but now we believe that they mean more – that they do have powers, that they represent a danger to the Fhoi Myore. And all here will agree on one thing, that the Bull of Crinanass has been seen in these parts.'

'This bull has been mentioned before.'

'Aye. A giant black bull which will kill any who seek to capture it, save one.'

'And is that one called Corum?' asked Corum with a smile.

'His name is not mentioned in the old texts. All the texts say is that he will bear the spear called Bryionak, clutched in a fist which shines like the moon.'

'And what is the spear Bryionak?'

'A magical spear, made by the Sidhi smith Goffanon and now again in his possession. You see, Prince Corum, after the Fhoi Myore came to Caer Llud and captured the High King, a warrior called Onragh, whose duty had been to protect the ancient treasures, fled with them in a chariot. But as he fled the treasures fell, one by one, from the chariot. Some were captured by pursuing Fhoi Myore, we heard. Others were found by Mabden. And the rest, if the rumours are to be trusted, were found by folk older than the Mabden or the Fhoi Myore – the Sidhi, whose gifts to us they originally were. We cast many runes and our wizards sought many oracles before we learned that the spear called Bryionak was once again in the possession of this mysterious Sidhi, the smith Goffanon.'

'And do you know where this smith dwells?'

'He is thought to dwell in a place now called Hy-Breasail, a mysterious island of enchantment lying south of our eastern shores. Our Druids believe that Hy-Breasail is all that remains of Lwym-an-Esh.'

'But the Fhoi Myore rule there, do they not?'

'They avoid the island. I know not why.'

'The danger must be great if they deserted a land that was once theirs.'

'My thinking also,' King Mannach agreed. 'But was the danger only apparent to the Fhoi Myore? No Mabden has ever returned from Hy-Breasail. The Sidhi are said to be blood relations to the Vadhagh. Of the same stock, many say. Perhaps only a Vadhagh could go to Hy-Breasail and return?'

Corum laughed aloud. 'Perhaps. Very well, King Mannach, I will go there and look for your magical spear.'

'You could go to your death.'

'Death is not what I fear, king.'

Soberly, King Mannach nodded. 'Aye. I believe I understand you, Prince Corum. And be reminded that there is much more to fear than death in these dark days of ours.'

The flames of the brands were burning low, guttering. The merry-making was now subdued. A single harpist played a soulful tune and sang a song of doomed lovers which Corum, in his drunkenness, identified with his own story, the story of himself and Rhalina. And it seemed to him, in the half-light, that the girl who had spoken to him earlier looked much like Rhalina. He stared at her as, unconscious of his gaze, she talked and laughed with one of the young warriors. And he began to hope. He hoped that somewhere in this world Rhalina had been reincarnated, that he would find her somewhere and, though she would not know him, she would fall in love with him as she had done before.

The girl turned her head and saw that he stared. She smiled at him, bowing slightly.

He raised his wine-cup, shouting somewhat wildly as he got to his feet. 'Sing on, bard, for I drink to my lost love Rhalina. And I pray that I shall find her in this grim world.'

And then he lowered his head, feeling that he had become foolish. The girl, seen properly, looked very little like Rhalina. But her eyes remained fixed on his as he sank back into his seat and, again, he stared at her with curiosity.

'I see you find my daughter worthy of your attention, Lord of the Mound,' came King Mannach's voice from beside Corum. The king spoke a little sardonically.

'Your daughter?'

'She is called Medhbh. Is she fair?'

'She is fair. She is fine, King Mannach.'

'She is my consort, since her mother was killed in our first fight with the Fhoi Myore. She is my right hand, my wisdom. A great battle-leader is Medhbh and our finest shot with battle-snare and the sling and tathlum.'

'What is the tathlum?'

'A hard ball, made from the ground-up brains and bones of our enemies. The Fhoi Myore fear it. That is why we use it. The brains and bones are mixed with lime and the lime sets hard. It seems an effective weapon against the invaders – and few weapons are effective, for their magic is strong.'

Corum said softly, as he sipped still more mead, 'Before I set off to find your spear for you, I should like very much to see the nature of our enemies.'

King Mannach smiled. 'It is a request we can easily grant, for two of the Fhoi Myore and their hunting packs have been seen not far from here. Our scouts believe that they head towards Caer Mahlod to attack our fort. They should be here by tomorrow's sunset.'

'You expect to beat them? You seem unconcerned.'

'We shall not beat them. Attacks such as this are, we think, more in the nature of a diversion for the Fhoi Myore. On some occasions they have succeeded in destroying one of our forts, but mainly they do this simply to unnerve us.'

'Then you will let me guest here until tomorrow's sunset?'

'Aye. If you promise to flee and seek Hy-Breasail if the fort begins to fall.'

'I promise,' said Corum.

Again he found himself glancing at King Mannach's daughter. She was laughing, flinging back her thick, red hair as she drained her mead-cup. He looked at her smooth limbs with their golden bangles, her firm, well-proportioned figure. She was the very picture of a warrior-princess, yet there was something else about her manner that made him think she was more than that. There was a fine intelligence in her eyes, and a sense of humour. Or did he imagine it all, wanting so desperately to find Rhalina in any Mabden woman?

At length he forced himself to leave the hall, to be escorted by King Mannach to the room set aside for him; a simple room, plainly furnished, with a wooden bed sprung with hide ropes, a straw mattress and furs to cover him against the cold. And he slept well in that bed and he did not dream at all.

Book Two

New foes, new friends, new
enigmas

1. SHAPES IN THE MIST

And the first morning dawned, and Corum saw the land.

Through the window, filled with oiled parchment to admit light and allow a shadowy view of the world outside, Corum saw that the walls and roofs of rocky Caer Mahlod sparkled with bright frost. Frost clung to grey granite stones. Frost hardened on the ground and frost made the trees, in the nearby forest below, bright and sharp and dead.

A log fire had burned in the low-roofed room Corum had been given, but now it was little more than warm ash. Corum shivered as he washed and donned his clothes.

And this, Corum thought, was spring in a place where once spring had been early and golden and winter barely noticed, an interval between the mellow days of autumn and the fresh mornings of the springtime.

Corum thought he recognised the landscape. He was not, in fact, far from the promontory on which Castle Erorn stood. The view through the oiled parchment window was further obscured by a suggestion of sea-mist rising from the other side of the fortress town, but far away could just be seen the outline of a crag which was almost certainly one of the crags close to Erorn. He conceived a wish to go to that point and see if Castle Erorn still stood and, if it did stand, if it was occupied by one who might know something of the castle's history. Before he left this part of the country he promised himself he would visit Castle Erorn, if only to witness a symbol of his own mortality.

Corum remembered the proud, laughing girl in the hall on the previous night. It was no betrayal of Rhalina, surely, if he admitted that he was attracted to the girl. And there had been little doubt that she had been attracted to him. Yet why did he feel so reluctant to admit the fact? Because he was afraid? How many women could he love and watch grow old and perish before his own long life was over? How many times could he feel the anguish of loss? Or would he begin to grow cynical, taking the women for a short while and leaving them before he could grow to love them too much? For their sake and for his, that might be the best solution to his profoundly tragic situation.

With a certain effort of will he dismissed the problem and the image of the red-haired daughter of the king. If today were a day for the making of war, then he had best concentrate on that matter before any other, lest the enemy silence his conscience when they silenced his breathing. He smiled, recalling King Mannach's words. The Fhoi Myore followed Death, Mannach had said. They courted Death. Well, was not the same true of Corum? And, if it were true, did that not make him the best enemy of the Fhoi Myore?

He left his chamber, ducking through the doorway, and walked through a series of small, round rooms until he reached the hall where he had dined the previous night. The hall was empty. Now the plate had been stored away and faint, grey light came reluctantly through the narrow windows to illuminate the hall. It was a cold place, and a stern one. A place, Corum thought, where men might kneel alone and purify their minds for battle. He flexed his silver hand, stretching the silver fingers, bending the silver knuckles, looking at the silver palm which was so detailed that every line of a natural hand was reproduced. The hand was attached by pins to the wrist-bone. Corum had performed the necessary operation himself, using his other hand to drive the drill through the bone. Well might anyone believe it to be a magic hand, so perfect a copy of the fleshly one was it. With a sudden gesture of distaste Corum let the hand fall to his side. It was the only thing he had created in two thirds of a century. The only work he had finished since the end of the adventure of the Sword Rulers.

He felt self-disgust and could not analyse the reason for the emotion. He began to pace back and forth over the great flagstones, sniffing at the cold, damp air like a hound impatient to begin the chase. Or was he so impatient to begin? Perhaps he was, instead, escaping from something. From the knowledge of his own, inevitable doom? The doom which Elric and Erekosë had both hinted at?

'Oh, by my ancestors, let the battle come and let it be a mighty one!' he shouted aloud. And, with a tense movement, he drew his battle-blade and whirled it, testing its temper, gauging its balance, before resheathing it with a crash which echoed through the hall.

'And let it be a successful one for Caer Mahlod, Sir Champion.' The voice was the sweet, amused voice of Medhbh, King Mannach's daughter, leaning in the doorway, a hand on her hip. Around her waist was a heavy belt bearing a sheathed dagger and broadsword. Her hair was tied back and she wore a sort of leather toga as her only armour. In her free hand she held a light helmet not unlike a Vadhagh helmet in design but made of brass.

Rarely given to bombastics and embarrassed at being discovered declaiming his confusion, Corum turned away, unable to look into her face. His humour left him momentarily. 'I fear you have very little of a hero in me, lady,' he said coldly.

'And a mournful god, Lord of the Mound. We hesitated, many of us, before summoning you to us. Many thought that, if you existed at all, you would be some dark and awful being of the Fhoi Myore kind, that we should release something horrible upon ourselves. But, no, we brought to us instead a man. And a man is much more complicated a being than a mere god. And our responsibilities, it seems, are different altogether – subtler and harder to accomplish. You are angry because I saw that you were fearful . . .'

'Perhaps it was not fear, lady.'

'But perhaps it was. You support our cause because you chose to. We have no claim on you. We have no power over you, as we thought we might have. You help us in spite of your fear and your self-doubt. That is worth much more than the help of some barely sensate supernatural creature such as the Fhoi Myore use. And the Fhoi Myore fear your legend, remember that, Prince Corum.'

Still Corum would not turn. Her kindness was unmistakable. Her sympathy was real. Her intelligence was as great as her beauty. How could he turn, when to turn would be to see her and to see her would be to love her helplessly, to love her as he had loved Rhalina.

Controlling his voice he said: 'I thank you for your kindness, lady. I will do what I can in the service of your folk, but I warn you to expect no spectacular aid from me.'

He did not turn for he did not trust himself. Did he see something of Rhalina in this girl because he needed Rhalina so much? And if that were the case what right had he to love Medhbh, herself, if he loved in her only qualities he imagined he saw?

Silver hand covered embroidered eye-patch, the cold and unfeeling fingers plucking at the fabric Rhalina had sewn. He almost shouted at her:

'And what of the Fhoi Myore? Do they come?'

'Not yet. Only the mist grows thicker. A sure sign of their presence somewhere near.'

'Does mist follow them?'

'Mist precedes them. Ice and snow follow. And the East Wind often signals their coming, bearing hailstones large as gulls' eggs. Ah, the earth dies and the trees bow when the Fhoi Myore march.' She spoke distantly.

The tension in the hall was increasing.

And then she said: 'You do not have to love me, lord.'

That was when he turned.

But she had gone.

Again he stared down at his metal hand, using the soft one, the one of flesh, to brush the tear from his single eye.

Faintly, from another, distant, part of the fortress, he thought he heard the strains of a Mabden harp playing music sweeter than any he had heard at Castle Erorn, and it was sad, the sound of that harp.

'You have a harpist of great genius in your Court, King Mannach.'

Corum and the king stood together on the outer walls of Caer Mahlod, looking to the east.

'You heard the harp, too?' King Mannach frowned. He was dressed in a breastplate of bronze with a bronze helmet upon his greying head. His handsome face was grim and his eyes puzzled. 'Some thought that you played it, Lord of the Mound.'

Corum held up his silver hand. 'This could not pluck such a strain as that.' He looked at the sky. 'It was a Mabden harpist I heard.'

'I think not,' said Mannach. 'At least, prince, it was no harpist of my Court we heard. The bards of Caer Mahlod prepare themselves for the fight. When they play, it will be martial songs we shall hear, not music like that which sounded this morning.'

'You did not recognise the tune?'

'I have heard it once before. In the grove of the mound, the first night that we came to call to you to help us. It was what encouraged us to believe that there might be truth in the legend. If that harp had not played, we should not have continued.'

Corum drew his brows together. 'Mysteries were never to my taste,' he said.

'Then life itself cannot be to your taste, lord.'

Corum smiled. 'I take your meaning, King Mannach. Nonetheless, I am suspicious of such things as ghostly harps.'

There was no more to say on the matter. King Mannach pointed towards the thick oak forest. Heavy mist clung to the topmost branches. Even as they watched, the mist seemed to grow denser, descending towards the ground until few of the frost-rimed trees could be seen. The sun was up, but its light was pale, for thin clouds were beginning to drift across it.

The day was still.

No birds sang in the forest. Even the movements of the warriors inside the fort were muted. When a man did shout, the sound seemed magnified and clear as a bell's note for a second before it was absorbed into the silence. All along the battlements had been stacked weapons – spears, arrows, bows, large stones and the round tathlum balls which would be flung from slings. Now the warriors began to take their places on the walls. Caer Mahlod was not a large settlement, but it was strong and heavy, squatting on the top of a hill whose sides had been smoothed so that it seemed like a man-made cone of enormous proportions. To the south and north stood several other cones like it and on two of these could be seen the ruins of other fortresses, suggesting that once Caer Mahlod had been part of a much larger settlement.

Corum turned to look towards the sea. There the mist had gone and the water was calm, blue and sparkling, as if the weather which touched the land did not extend across the ocean. And now Corum could see that he had been right in judging Castle Erorn nearby. Two or three miles to the south was the familiar outline of the promontory and what might be the remains of a tower.

'Do you know that place, King Mannach?' asked Corum, pointing.

'It is called Castle Owyn by us, for it resembles a castle when seen from the distance, but really it is a natural formation. Some legends are attached to it concerning its occupation by supernatural beings – by the Sidhi, by Cremm Croich. But the only architect of Castle Owyn was the wind and the only mason the sea.'

'Yet I should like to go there,' said Corum. 'When I can.'

'If both of us survive the raid of the Fhoi Myore – indeed, if the Fhoi Myore decide not to attack us – then I will take you. But there is nothing to see, Prince Corum. The place is best observed from this distance.'

'I suspect,' said Corum, 'that you are right, king.'

Now, as they spoke, the mist grew thicker still and obscured all sight of the sea. Mist fell upon Caer Mahlod and filled her narrow streets. Mist moved upon the fortress from all sides save the west.

Even the small sounds in the fort died as the occupants waited to discover what the mist had brought with it.

It had become dark, almost like evening. It had become cold so that Corum, more warmly clothed than any of the others, shivered and drew his scarlet robe more tightly about him.

And there came the howling of a hound from out of the mist. A savage, desolate howling which was taken up by other canine throats until it filled the air on all sides of the fortress called Caer Mahlod.

Peering through his single eye, Corum tried to see the hounds themselves. For an instant he thought he saw a pale, slinking shape at the bottom of the hill, below the walls. Then the shape had gone. Corum carefully strung his long, bone bow and nocked a slender arrow to the string. Grasping the shaft of the bow with his metal hand, he used his fleshly hand to draw back the string to his cheek and he waited until he saw another faint shape appear before he let fly.

The arrow pierced the mist and vanished.

A scream rose high and horrible and became a snarl, a growl. Then a shape was running up the hill towards the fort. It ran very fast and very straight. Two yellow eyes glared directly into Corum's face as if the beast recognised instinctively the source of its wound. Its long, feathery tail waved as it ran and at first it seemed it had another tail, rigid and thin, but then Corum realised that it was his arrow, sticking from the animal's side, which he saw. He nocked another arrow to his bowstring. He drew the string back and glared, himself, into the beast's blazing eyes. A red mouth gaped and yellow fangs dripped saliva. The hair was coarse and shaggy and, as the dog approached, Corum realised it was as large as a small pony.

The sound of its snarling filled his ears and still he did not let fly, for it was sometimes hard to see against the background of mist.

Corum had not expected the hound to be white. A glowing whiteness which was somehow disgusting to look upon. Only the ears of the hound were darker than the rest of its body and these ears were a glistening red, the colour of fresh blood.

Higher and higher up the hill raced the white hound, the first arrow bouncing apparently unnoticed in its side, and its howl seemed almost to be a howl of obscene laughter as it anticipated sinking its fangs into Corum's throat. There was glee in the yellow eyes.

Corum could wait no longer. He released the arrow.

The shaft seemed to travel very slowly towards the white hound. The beast saw the arrow and tried to side-step, but it had been running too fast, too purposefully, its movements were not properly coordinated and as it ducked to save its right eye, its legs tangled and it received the arrow in its left eye with such an impact that the tip of the arrow burst through the other side of the skull.

The hound opened its great jaws as it collapsed, but no further sound escaped that frightful throat. It fell, rolled a short way down the hill, and was still.

Corum let out a sigh and turned to speak to King Mannach.

But King Mannach was already flinging back his arm, aiming a spear into the mist where at least a hundred pale shadows skulked and slavered and wailed their determination to be revenged upon the slayers of their sibling.

2. THE FIGHT AT CAER MAHLOD

'Oh, there are many!'

King Mannach's expression was troubled as he took up a second spear and flung that after the first. 'More than any I have seen before.' He glanced round to see how his men fared. Now all were active against the hounds. They whirled slings, shot arrows and threw spears. The hounds surrounded Caer Mahlod. 'There are many. Perhaps the Fhoi Myore have already heard that you have come to us, Prince Corum. Perhaps they have determined to destroy you.'

Corum made no reply, for he had seen a huge white hound slinking at the very foot of the wall, sniffing the entrance way which had been blocked with a large boulder. Leaning out over the battlements Corum let fly with one of his last arrows, striking the beast in the back of its skull. It moaned and ran off into the mist. Corum could not see if he had killed it. They were hard to kill, these hounds. Hard to see in the mist and the frost, save for their blood-red ears, their yellow eyes.

Even had they been darker it would have been difficult to fight them. The mist grew thicker still. It attacked the throats and the eyes of the defenders so that they were constantly wiping the stuff from their faces, spitting over the walls at the hounds as they tried to free their lungs of the cold and clogging dampness. Yet they were brave. They did not falter. Spear after spear darted down. Arrow after arrow arced into the ranks of those sinister dogs. Only the piles of tathlum balls were not used and Corum was curious to know why, for King Mannach had not had time to tell him. But spears and arrows and rocks were already running low and only a few of the pale dogs were dead.

Kerenos, whoever he might be, had well-stocked kennels, thought Corum as he shot the last of his arrows, dropped his bow and pulled his sword from its scabbard.

And their howling brought tension to every nerve so that one had to fight one's own cringing muscles as well as the dogs themselves.

King Mannach ran along the battlements encouraging his warriors. So far none had fallen. Only when the missiles were no more would they be forced to defend themselves with their blades, with their axes and their pikes. That time was almost upon them.

Corum paused to draw a breath and try to take account of their situation. There were something less than a hundred hounds below. There were something more than a hundred men on the battlements. The hounds would have to make enormous leaps to get a foothold on the walls. That they were capable of making such leaps, Corum was in no doubt.

Even as he considered this he saw a white beast come flying towards him, its forelegs outstretched, its jaws snapping, its hot, yellow eyes glaring. If he had not already unsheathed his blade he would have been slain there and then. But now he brought the sword up, stabbing out at the hound even as it flew through the air towards him. He caught it in the belly and he nearly lost his footing as the thing impaled itself upon the point of his sword, grunted as if in mild surprise, growled as it understood its fate, and made one feeble, futile snap at him before it went tumbling backwards to fall directly upon the spine of one of its fellows.

For a little while Corum thought that the Hounds of Kerenos had had enough of battle for that day, for they seemed to retreat. But their growlings, their mutterings, their occasional howlings, made it plain that they were simply resting, biding their time, preparing for the next attack. Perhaps they were taking instructions from an unseen master – perhaps Kerenos himself. Corum would have given much for a glimpse of the Fhoi Myore. He wanted to see at least one, if only to form his own opinion of what they were and from where they derived their powers. A little earlier he had seen a darker shape in the mist, a shape which was taller than the hounds and had seemed to walk on two legs, but the mist was shifting so rapidly all the time (though never dispersing) that he might have been deceived. If he had actually seen the outline of a Fhoi Myore, then there was no doubt that they were considerably taller than Men and probably not of the same race at all. Yet where could others, not Vadhagh, Nhadragh or Mabden, have come from? This had puzzled Corum ever since his first conversation with King Mannach.

'The hounds! 'Ware the hounds!'

A warrior shouted as he was borne backward by a gleaming white shape which had flown silently at him from out of the mist. Hound and man went together off the walls and fell with a terrific crack into the street below.

Only the hound got up, its jaws full of the warrior's flesh. It grinned, turned and loped into the street. Barely thinking, Corum flung his sword at it and struck it in the side. It shrieked and tried to snap at the sword protruding from between its ribs, just as a puppy might chase its own tail. Four or five rotations the great hound made before it understood that it was dead.

Corum bounded down the steps to the street to retrieve his sword. He had never seen such monstrous dogs before, neither could he understand their strange colouring, which was like nothing else in nature he had ever seen. With distaste he tugged his blade free from the massive carcass, wiping the blood on the pale, coarse fur. Then he ran back up the steps to take his place on the wall.

For the first time he noticed the stink. It was definitely a canine stink, like the smell of wet, dirty hair, but for a few seconds at a time it could be almost overpowering. With the mist attacking eyes and mouths and the stink of the hounds attacking their nostrils, the defenders were being hard-pressed to accomplish their work. Dogs were on the walls now in several places and four warriors lay with their throats torn out, while two of the Hounds of Kerenos were also dead, one with its head hacked clean off.

Corum was beginning to tire and judged that the others must also be wearying. In an ordinary battle they would have had every right to be exhausted by now, but here they did not fight men but beasts and the allies of the beasts were the elements themselves.

Corum leaped to one side as a hound – one of the largest he had so far seen – cleared the battlements behind him and landed on the platform beyond, hissing and panting, its eyes rolling, its tongue lolling, its fangs dripping. The smell choked Corum. It issued from the mouth of the beast, a fetid, unhealthy smell. Growling softly, the hound gathered itself to attack Corum, the strange red ears lying flat against the tapering skull.

Corum shouted something, grabbed up his own long-hafted war-axe from where he had kept it by the wall, and whirling this weapon ran at the hound.

The hound cringed perceptibly as the blade flashed over its white head. Its tail began to sink between its legs before it realised that it was considerably heavier and stronger than Corum and drew back its lips in a snarl exposing teeth some twelve inches long.

Bringing the war-axe round for a second swing, Corum was caught off balance and the hound charged before the axe could come back. Corum had to take three rapid paces away from the beast as it flung itself at him, to allow the axe to continue its swing and thud into the hound's hind-leg, crippling it but not stopping it. Corum was close to the edge and knew that a leap might break his legs at very least. One more step backward would be enough to send him falling into the street. There was only one thing he could do. As the hound charged at him, he sidestepped and ducked and the dog went sailing past him and smashed head-first on to the cobbles, breaking its neck.

Now the noise of battle came from every part of the fortress, for several Hounds of Kerenos had gained access to the streets and were roaming those, sniffing for the old women and children who huddled behind the barricaded doors.

Medhbh, King Mannach's daughter, had been in charge of the streets and Corum glimpsed her running at the head of a handful of warriors, charging upon two of the hounds who had found themselves trapped in a street with no exit. Some of her red hair had come loose from her helmet and it flew as she ran. Her lithe figure, the speed and control of her movements, her evident courage, astonished Corum. He had never known a woman like this Medhbh – or, indeed, other women here who fought with their men and who shared equal duties with them. Such beautiful women, too, thought Corum; and then he cursed himself for his lack of attention, for another beast came leaping and snapping and howling at him and he whirled his war-axe and he shouted his Vadhagh war-cry and he smashed the blade deep into the hound's skull, between its red, tufted ears, and he wished that the fight would end, for he was so weary that he could not believe he could slay another of the dogs.

The baying of those dreadful beasts seemed to grow louder and louder, the stink of their breath made Corum wish for the harshness of the mist in his lungs, and still the white bodies flew through the air and landed upon the battlements, still the great fangs snapped and the yellow eyes blazed, still men died as the jaws ripped flesh, sinew and bone. And Corum leaned against the wall and panted and panted and knew that the next dog to attack him would kill him. He had no intention of resisting. He was finished. He would die here and all problems would be solved in an instant, Caer Mahlod would fall. The Fhoi Myore would rule.

Something made him look down into the street again.

There was Medhbh, standing alone, sword in hand, while a massive hound rushed at her. The rest of her party were all down. Their torn corpses could be seen strewn across the cobbles. Only Medhbh remained and she would perish soon.

Corum had jumped before he knew that he had made up his mind. His booted feet landed full on the rump of the great hound, bringing its hind parts to the ground. The war-axe whistled now and crunched through the bone of the huge dog's vertebrae, almost chopping the beast in two. And Corum, carried forward by his own momentum, fell across the corpse, slipped in the beast's blood, struck his skull against its broken spine and fell over on to his back, desperately trying to regain his footing. Even Medhbh had not realised what had happened, for she had struck at one of the dog's eyes with her sword, not realising that the creature was already dead, before she saw Corum.

She grinned as he got to his feet and began to tug his war-axe from the corpse.

'So you would not see me dead, then, my elven prince.'

'Lady,' said Corum, gasping for breath, 'I would not.'

He freed his axe and staggered back up the steps to the battlements where weary warriors did their best to meet the attacks of seemingly innumerable hounds.

Corum forced himself forward, to help a warrior who was about to go down before one of the dogs. His axe was becoming blunt with all the slaughter and this time his blow only stunned the dog which recovered almost immediately and turned on him. But a pike took it in the belly and the worst Corum got was the thing's thick and ill-smelling blood pouring over his breastplate.

He stumbled away, peering through the mist beyond the walls. And this time he did see a looming shape – a gigantic figure of a man, apparently with antlered horns growing from the sides of its head, its face all misshapen, its body all warped, raising something to its lips, as if to drink.

And then came a sound which made all the hounds stop dead in their tracks and caused the surviving warriors to drop their weapons and cover their ears.

It was a sound full of horror, part laughter, part screaming, part agonised wail, part triumphant shout. It was the sound of the Horn of Kerenos, calling back his hounds.

Corum glimpsed the figure again as it disappeared into the mist. The hounds which remained alive instantly began to dive over the walls and run back down the hill until there was not a single living dog remaining in Caer Mahlod.

Then the mist began to lift, rushing back towards the forest as if drawn behind Kerenos like a cloak.

Once more the Horn sounded.

Some men were vomiting, so terrible was the sound. Some men screamed, while others sobbed.

Yet it was plain that Kerenos and his pack had had enough sport for that day. They had shown the people of Caer Mahlod a little of their power. It was all they had wanted to do. Corum could almost understand that the Fhoi Myore might see the battle in terms of a friendly passage of arms before the main fight began.

The fight at Caer Mahlod had brought about the deaths of some four and thirty hounds.

Fifty warriors had died, men and women both.

'Quickly, Medhbh, the tathlum!'

King Mannach, wounded in the shoulder and bleeding still, cried to his daughter. She had put one of the round balls of brains and lime into her sling and was whirling it.

She let fly into the mist, after Kerenos himself.

King Mannach knew she had not hit the Fhoi Myore.

'It is one of the few things they believe will kill them, the tathlum,' he said.

Quietly they left the walls of Caer Mahlod and went to mourn their dead.

'Tomorrow,' said Corum, 'I will set off upon this quest to find your spear Bryionak for you and bring it to you, clutched in my silver hand. I will do all that I can to save the folk of Caer Mahlod from the likes of Kerenos and his hounds. I will go.'

King Mannach, aided down the steps by his daughter, merely nodded his head, for he was very faint.

'But first I must go to this place you call Castle Owyn,' said Corum. 'That I must do first, before I leave.'

'I will take you there this evening,' said Medhbh.

And Corum did not refuse.

3. A MOMENT IN THE RUINS

Now that it was late afternoon and the cloud had dropped away from the face of the sun which had melted the frost a little and warmed the day and brought traces of the odour of spring to the landscape, Corum and the warrior princess Medhbh, nicknamed 'of the Long Arm' for her skill with snare and tathlum, rode horses out to the place which Corum called Erorn and she called Olwyn.

Though it was spring, there was no foliage on the trees and barely any grass growing upon the ground. It was a stark world, this world. Life was fleeing it. Corum remembered how lush it had been, even when he had left. It depressed him to think what so much of the country must look like after the Fhoi Myore, their hounds and their servants, had visited it.

They reined their horses near the edge of the cliff and looked at the sea muttering and gasping on the shingle of the tiny bay.

Tall black cliffs – old cliffs and crumbling – rose out of the water and the cliffs were full of caves, as Corum had known them at least a millennium before.

The promontory, however, had changed. Part of it had fallen at the centre, collapsing into the sea in a tumble of rotting

63

granite, and now Corum knew why little of Castle Erorn remained.

'There is what they call the Sidhi Tower – or Cremm's Tower – see.' Medhbh showed him what she meant. It lay on the other side of the chasm created by the falling rock. 'It looks man-made from a distance, but it is really nature's work.'

But Corum knew better. He recognised the worn lines. True they seemed the work of nature, for Vadhagh building had always tended to blend into the landscape. That was why, in his own time, some travellers even failed to realise that Castle Erorn was there.

'It is the work of my folk,' he said quietly. 'That is the remains of Vadhagh architecture, though none would believe it, I know.'

She was surprised. She laughed. 'So the legend has truth in it. It *is* your tower!'

'I was born there,' said Corum. He sighed. 'And, I suppose, I died there, too,' he added. Leaving his horse he walked to the edge of the cliff and looked down. The sea had made a narrow channel through the gap. He looked across at the remains of the tower. He remembered Rhalina and he remembered his family, his father Prince Khlonskey, his mother the Princess Colatalarna, his sisters Ilastru and Pholhinra, his uncle Prince Rhanan, his cousin Sertreda. All dead now, Rhalina at least had lived her natural lifespan, but the others had been brutally slain by Glan-dyth-a-Krae and his murderers. Now none remembered them save Corum. For a moment he envied them, for too many remembered Corum.

'But you live,' she said simply.

'Do I? I wonder if perhaps I am no more than a shade, a figment of your folk's desires. Already my memories of my past life grow dim. I can barely remember how my family looked.'

'You have a family – where you come from?'

'I know that the legend says that I slept in the mound until I was needed, but that is not true. I was brought here from my own time – when Castle Erorn stood where ruins stand now. Ah, there have been so many ruins in my life. . . .'

'And your family is there? You left it to help us?'

Corum shook his head and turned to look at her, smiling a bitter smile.

'No, lady, I would not have done that. My family was slain by your race – by Mabden. My wife died.' He hesitated.

'Slain, too?'

'Of old age.'

'She was older than you?'

'No.'

'You are truly immortal, then?' She looked down at the distant sea.

'As far as it matters, yes. That is why I fear to love, you see.'

'I would not fear that.'

'Neither did the Margravine Rhalina, my bride. And I think I did not fear it, for I could not experience it until it happened. But when I experienced the loss of her I thought I could never bear that emotion again.'

A single gull appeared from nowhere and perched on a nearby spur of rock. There had been many gulls here once.

'You will never feel that exact emotion again, Corum.'

'True. And yet . . .'

'You love corpses?'

He was offended. 'That is cruel. . . .'

'What is left of dead people is the corpse. And if you do not love corpses, then you must find someone living to love.'

He shook his head. 'Is it so simple to you, lovely Medhbh?'

'I did not think that I said something simple, Lord Corum of the Mound.'

He made an impatient gesture with his silver hand. 'I am not of the Mound. I do not like the implications of that title. You speak of corpses – that title makes me feel like a corpse that has been resurrected. I can smell the mould on my clothes when you speak of "the Lord of the Mound".'

'The older legends said you drank blood. There were sacrifices on the mound during the darker times.'

'I have no taste for blood.' His mood was lifting. The experience of the fight with the Hounds of Kerenos had helped rid him of some of his gloomy thoughts and replaced them with

65

more practical considerations.

And now he was reaching out to touch her face, to trace, with his hand of flesh, the line of her lips, her neck, her shoulder.

And now they were embracing and he was weeping and full of joy.

They kissed. They made love near the ruins of Castle Erorn while the sea pounded in the bay below. And then they lay in the last of the sunshine, looking out to sea.

'Listen.' Medhbh raised her head, her hair floating about her face.

He heard it. He had heard it a little while before she mentioned it, but he had not wanted to hear it.

'A harp,' she said. 'What sweet music it plays. How melancholy it is, that music. Do you hear it?'

'Yes.'

'It is familiar. . . .'

'Perhaps you heard it this morning, just before the attack?' He spoke reluctantly, distantly.

'Perhaps. And in the grove of the mound.'

'I know – just before your folk tried to summon me for the first time.'

'Who is the harpist? What is the music?'

Corum was looking across the gulf at the ruined tower that was all that remained of Castle Erorn. Even to his eyes it did not look mortal-built. Perhaps, after all, the wind and the sea had carved the tower and his memories were false.

He was afraid.

She, too, now stared at the tower.

'That is where the music comes from,' he said. 'The harp plays the music of time.'

4. THE WORLD TURNED WHITE

Garbed in fur, Corum set forth.

He wore a white fur robe over his own clothes and there was a huge hood on the robe to cover his helmet, all made from the soft pelt of the winter marten. Even the horse they had given him had a coat of fur-trimmed doeskin embroidered with scenes of a valiant past. They gave him fur-lined boots and gauntlets of doeskin, also embroidered, and a high saddle and saddle-panniers and soft cases for his bow, his lances and the blade of his war-axe. He wore one of the gauntlets on his silver hand, so that no casual eye would know him. And he kissed Medhbh and he saluted the folk of Caer Mahlod as they stood regarding him with grave and hopeful eyes upon the walls of the fortress town and was kissed upon his forehead by King Mannach.

'Bring us back our spear Bryionak,' said King Mannach, 'so that we may tame the bull, the Black Bull of Crinanass, so that we may defeat our enemies and make our land green again.'

'I will seek it,' promised Prince Corum Jhaelen Irsei, and his single eye shone brightly, with tears or with confidence, none could tell. And he mounted his great horse, the huge and heavy war-horse of the Tuha-na-Cremm Croich, and he placed his feet in the stirrups he had had them make for him (for they had forgotten the use of stirrups) and he put his tall lance in the stirrup rest, though he did not unfurl his banner, stitched for him all the previous night by the maidens of Caer Mahlod.

'You look a great war-knight, my lord,' murmured Medhbh and he reached down to stroke her red-gold hair and touch her soft cheek.

He said: 'I will return, Medhbh.'

He had ridden south-east for two days and the riding had not been difficult, for he had ridden this way more than once and time had not destroyed many of the landmarks that had once been familiar to him. Perhaps because he had found so little and yet so much at Castle Erorn he now headed for Moidel's Mount where Rhalina's castle had stood once. It was easy to justify this goal in terms of his quest, for Moidel's Mount had once been the last outpost of Lwym-an-Esh and now the last of Lwym-an-Esh was Hy-Breasail. He would lose neither time nor direction by seeking out Moidel's Mount, if that had not, too, sunk when Lwym-an-Esh sank.

South and east he rode and the world grew colder and showers of bright, bouncing hailstones capered on the hard earth, pattered on his armoured shoulders and his horse's neck and withers. Many times his road across the great, wild moor was obscured by sheets of this frozen rain and sometimes it grew so bad that he was forced to take shelter where he could, usually behind a boulder, for there were few trees on the moor, save some gorse and stunted birch, and all the bracken and heather, which should have been flourishing at this season, was either completely dead or feebly alive. Once deer and pheasant had been everywhere but now Corum saw no pheasant and had seen only one wary stag, thin, mad-eyed, on the whole of his journey. And the farther east he rode, the worse the prospect of the land became, and soon there was heavy frost sparkling on every piece of vegetation, and coverings of snow on every hill-top, on every boulder. The land rose higher and the air grew thinner and colder and Corum was glad of the heavy robe his friends had given him, for slowly the frost gave way to snow and every way he looked the world was white and its whiteness reminded him of the colour of the Hounds of Kerenos, and now his horse waded through snow up to its hocks and Corum knew that, if attacked, he would have great difficulty in fleeing any danger and almost as much in manoeuvring to face it. But at least the skies remained blue and sharp and clear and the sun, though giving little heat, was bright. It was the mist which made Corum wary, for he knew that with the mist might come the devil hounds and their masters.

And now he began to discover the shallow valleys of the moors and in the valleys the hamlets, the villages and the towns where once Mabden folk had lived. And every settlement was deserted.

Corum took to using these deserted places for his night camps. Hesitant to build a fire lest the smoke be seen by enemies or potential enemies, he found that he could burn peat on the flagstones of empty cottages in a manner which would let the smoke disperse before it could be detected from even a close distance. Thus he was able to keep both his horse and himself warm and cook hot food. Without these comforts his ride would have been miserable indeed.

What saddened him was that the cottages still contained the furniture, ornaments and little trinkets of the folk who had lived in them. There had been no looting for, Corum imagined, the Fhoi Myore had no interest in Mabden artefacts, but in some of the villages, the most easterly, there were signs that the Hounds of Kerenos had come a-hunting and found no shortage of prey. Doubtless that was why so many had fled and sought safety in the old, disused hill-forts like Caer Mahlod.

Corum could tell that a complex and reasonably sophisticated culture had flourished here, a rich, agricultural people who had had time to develop their artistic gifts. In the abandoned settlements he found books as well as paintings, musical instruments as well as elegant metalwork and pottery. It saddened him to see it all. Had his battle against the Sword Rulers been pointless, then? Lwym-an-Esh, which he had fought for as much as he had fought for his own folk, was gone and what had followed it was now destroyed.

After a while he began to avoid the villages and seek out caves where he would not be reminded of the Mabden tragedy.

But then, one morning, after he had been riding for little more than an hour, he came to a broad depression in the moor, in the centre of which was a frozen tarn. To the north-east of the tarn he saw what he at first took to be standing stones, all about the height of a man, but there were several hundred whereas most stone circles were usually made up of hardly more than a score of granite slabs. As with everywhere else on this moor, snow was thick and snow covered the stones.

Corum's path took him the other side of the tarn and he was about to avoid the monuments (for such he judged them) when he thought he caught a movement of something black against the universal whiteness. A crow? He shaded his eyes to peer among the stones. No, something larger. A wolf, possibly. If it were a deer, he had need of meat. He drew the cover off his bow and strung it, swinging his lance behind him to give him a clear shot as he fitted an arrow to the string. Then, with his heels, he urged his horse forward.

As he drew closer he began to realise that these standing stones were not typical. The carving on them was much more detailed, so much so that they resembled the finest Vadhagh statuary. And that was what they were – statues of men and women poised as if in battle. Who had made them and for what purpose?

Again Corum saw the movement of a dark shape. Then it was hidden again by the statues. Corum found something familiar about the statues. Had he seen work like them before?

Then he recalled his adventure in Arioch's castle and slowly the truth came. Corum resisted the truth. He did not want to know it.

But now he was close to the nearest of the statues and he could not avoid the evidence.

These were not statues at all.

These were the corpses of folk very much like the tall, fair folk of Tuha-na-Cremm Croich; corpses frozen as they prepared to do battle against an enemy. Corum could see their expressions, their attitudes. He saw the look of resolute courage on every face – men, women, quite young boys and girls – the javelins, axes, swords, bows, slings and knives still clutched in their hands. They had come to do battle with the Fhoi Myore and the Fhoi Myore had answered their courage with this – this expression of contempt for their power and their nobility. Not even the Hounds of Kerenos had come against this sad army; perhaps the Fhoi Myore themselves had refused to appear, sending only a coldness – a sudden, awful coldness which had worked instantly and turned warm flesh into ice.

Corum turned away from the sight, the bow forgotten in his hands. The horse was nervous and was only too glad to bear him away around the banks of the frozen tarn where stiff, dead reeds stood like stalagmites, like a travesty of the dead folk nearby. And Corum saw two who had been wading in the water and they too were frozen, appearing to be chopped off at the waist by the flat ice, their arms raised in attitudes of terror. A boy and a girl, both probably little older than sixteen years.

The landscape was dead. The landscape was silent. The plodding of the horse's hooves sounded to Corum like the tolling of a death-knell. He fell forward across his saddle-pommel, refusing to look, unable even to weep, so horror-struck was he by the images he had seen.

Then he heard a moan which at first he thought was his own. He lifted his head, drawing cold air into his lungs, and he heard the sound again. He turned. He forced himself to glance back at the frozen host, judging that to be the direction from where the moan had come.

A black shape was clearly visible now among the white ones. A black cloak flapped like the broken wing of a raven.

'Who are you?' Corum cried, 'that you weep for these?'

The figure was kneeling. As Corum called out, it rose to its feet, but no face or even limbs could be seen emerging from the tattered cloak.

'Who are you?' Corum turned his horse.

'Take me, too, Fhoi Myore vassal!' The voice was weary and it was old. 'I know you and I know your cause.'

'I think that you do not know me, then,' said Corum kindly. 'Now, say who you are, old woman.'

'I am Ieveen, mother of some of these, wife of one of these, and I deserve to die. If you be enemy, slay me. If you be friend. then slay me, friend, and prove thyself a good friend to Ieveen. I would go, now, where my lost ones go. I want no more of this world and its cruelties. I want no more visions and terrors and truths. I am Ieveen and I prophesied all that you see and that is why I fled when they would not listen to me. And when I came back, I found that I had been right. And that is why I weep – but not for these. I weep for myself and my betrayal of my folk. I am Ieveen the Seeress, but now I have none to see for, none to respect me, least of all myself. The Fhoi Myore came and they struck them down. The Fhoi Myore left, in their clouds, with their dogs, hunting more satisfactory game than my poor clan who were so brave, who believed that the Fhoi Myore, no matter how depraved, how wicked, would respect them enough to offer them a fair fight. I warned them of what would befall them. I begged them to flee as I fled. They were reasonable. They told me I could go but they wished to stay, that a folk must keep its pride or perish in different ways, each one dying within themselves. I did not understand them. Now I understand them. So slay me, sir.'

Now the thin arms were raised imploringly, the black rags falling away from flesh that was blue with cold and with age. Now the head covering dropped and the wrinkled face with its thin, grey hair was revealed, and Corum saw the eyes and wondered if, in all his travels, he had ever seen such misery as that which he saw in the face of Ieveen the Seeress.

'Slay me, sir!'

'I cannot,' said Corum. 'If I had more courage I would do what you ask, but I have no courage of that sort, lady.' He pointed westward with his bow which was still strung. 'Go that way and try to reach Caer Mahlod, where your folk still resist the Fhoi Myore. Tell them of this. Warn them of this. And thus you will redeem yourself in your own eyes. You are

72

already redeemed in mine.'

'Caer Mahlod? You come from there? From Cremms-mound and the coast?'

'I am upon a quest. I seek a spear.'

'The spear Bryionak?' Her voice now had a peculiar gasp in it. The tone was higher. And her eyes were now looking out beyond Corum as she swayed a little. 'Bryionak and the Bull of Crinanass. Silver hand. Cremm Croich shall come. Cremm Croich shall come. Cremm Croich shall come.' The voice had changed again to a soft chant. The lines seemed to leave her old face and a certain beauty was there now. 'Cremm Croich shall come and he shall be called – called – called . . . And his name shall not be his name.'

Corum had been about to speak but now he listened in fascination as the old seeress continued to chant.

'Corum Llaw Ereint. Silver hand and scarlet robe. Corum is thy name and ye shall be slain by a brother. . . .'

Corum had begun to believe in the old woman's powers, but now he found himself smiling. 'Slain I might be, old woman, but not by a brother. I have no brother.'

'Ye have many brothers, prince. I see them all. Proud champions all. Great heroes.'

Corum felt his heart begin to beat faster and there was a tightness in his stomach. He said hastily: 'No brothers, old woman. None.' Why did he fear what she said? What did she know that he refused to know?

'You are afraid,' she said. 'Then I see that I speak truth. But do not fear. You have only three things to fear. The first is the brother, of which I spoke. The second is a harp. And the third is beauty. Fear those three things, Corum Llaw Ereint, but nothing else.'

'Beauty? The other two are at least tangible – but why fear beauty?'

'And the third is beauty,' she said again. 'Fear those three things.'

'I'll listen to this nonsense no more. You have my sympathy, old woman. Your ordeal has turned your mind. Go, as I said, to Caer Mahlod and there they will look after you. There you can atone for what makes you guilty, though I say again that you should not feel guilt. Now I must continue my quest for the spear Bryionak.'

'Bryionak, Sir Champion, will be yours. But first you will make a bargain.'

'A bargain? With whom?'

'I know not. I take your advice. If I live, I will tell the folk of Caer Mahlod of what I have seen here. But you must take my advice, also, Corum Jhaelen Irsei. Do not dismiss my advice. I am Ieveen the Seeress and what I see is always true. It is only the consequences of my own actions that I cannot foresee. That is my fate.'

'And it is my fate, I think,' said Corum as he rode away from her, 'to flee from truth. At least,' he added, 'I think I prefer small truths to larger ones. Farewell, old woman.'

Surrounded by her frozen sons, her ragged cloak fluttering about her old, thin body, her voice high and faint, she called once more to him:

'Fear only those three things, Corum of the Silver Hand. Brother, harp and beauty.'

Corum wished that the harp had not been mentioned. The other two things he could easily dismiss for a mad woman's ravings. But he had already heard the harp. And he already feared it.

5. THE WIZARD CALATIN

Bowed and broken by the weight of the snow, its trees without leaves, without berries, its animal inhabitants dead or fled, the forest had lost its strength.

Corum had known this forest. It was the Forest of Laahr where he had first awakened after being mutilated by Glandyth-a-Krae. Reflectively he looked at his left hand, the silver hand, and he touched his right eye, recalling the Brown Man of Laahr and the Giant of Laahr. Really the Giant of Laahr had begun all this, first by saving his life, then by . . . He dismissed the thoughts. On the far side of the Forest of Laahr was the westerly tip of this land and at that tip Moidel's Mount had stood.

He shook his head as he looked at the ruined forest. There would be no Pony Tribes living there now. No Mabden to plague him.

Again he recalled the evil Glandyth. Why did evil always come from the eastern shores? Was it some special doom that this land had to suffer, through cycle upon cycle of history?

And so, with such idle speculation consuming his thoughts, Corum rode into the snowy tangle of the forest.

Dark and bleak, the oaks, the alders, the elms and the

quickens stretched on all sides of him now. And of the trees in the forest, only the yews seemed to be bearing the burden of the snow with any fortitude. Corum recalled the reference to the People of the Pines. Could it be true that the Fhoi Myore slew broadleaf trees and left only the conifers? What reason could they have for destroying mere trees? How could trees be a threat to them?

Shrugging, Corum continued his ride. It was not an easy ride. Huge drifts of snow had banked up everywhere and elsewhere trees had cracked and fallen, one upon the other, so that he was forced to make wide circles around them, until he was in great danger of losing his way.

But he forced himself to continue, praying that beyond the forest, where the sea was, the weather would improve.

For two days Corum plunged on through the Forest of Laahr until he admitted to himself that he was completely lost.

The cold, it was true, seemed just a little less intense, but that was no real indication that he was heading west. It was quite possible that he had simply grown used to it.

But, warmer though it might be, the journey had become gruelling. At night he had to clear away the snow to sleep and he had long since forgotten his earlier caution concerning the lighting of fires. A big fire was the easiest way of melting the snow and he hoped that the snow-heavy tree boughs would disperse the smoke enough so that it would not be seen from the edge of the forest.

He camped one night in a small clearing, built his fire of dead branches, using melted snow to water his horse and searching beneath the snow for a few surviving blades of grass on which the beast might feed, and had begun to feel the benefit of the flames upon his frozen bones, when he thought he detected a familiar howling coming from the depths of the forest in what he took to be the north. Instantly he got up, hurling handfuls of snow upon the fire to extinguish it, and listening carefully for the sound to come again.

It came.

It was unmistakable. There were at least a dozen canine throats baying in unison, and the only throats which could make that particular sound belonged to the hunting dogs of the Fhoi Myore, the Hounds of Kerenos.

Corum got his bow and quiver of arrows from where he had stacked them with the rest of his gear when unsaddling his horse. The nearest tree to him was an ancient oak. It had not completely died and he guessed that its branches would probably support his weight. He tied his lances together with a cord, put the cord between his teeth, cleared snow as best he could from the lower branches and began to climb.

Slipping and almost falling twice he got as high as he could and, by carefully shaking the branches, managed to clear some of the snow so that he could see into the glade below without being easily seen himself.

He had hoped that the horse might try to escape when it scented the hounds, but it was too well trained. It waited trustingly for him, cropping the sparse grass. He heard the hounds come closer. He was now almost sure that they had detected him. He hung the quiver on a branch within easy reach of his hand and selected an arrow. He could hear the dogs, now, crashing through the forest. The horse snorted and flattened its ears, its eyes rolling as it looked this way and that for its master.

Now Corum saw mist beginning to form on the edges of the glade. He thought he detected a white, slinking shape. He began to draw back the bowstring, lying flat along the branch and bracing himself with his feet.

The first hound, its red tongue lolling, its red ears twitching, its yellow eyes hot with bloodlust, entered the glade. Corum sighted along the shaft of the arrow, aiming for the heart.

He released the string. There was a thud as the string struck his gauntleted wrist. A twang as the bow straightened. The arrow flew directly to its target. Corum saw the hound stagger and reel, staring at the arrow protruding from its side. Plainly, it had no idea from where the deadly missile had come. Its legs buckled. Corum reached for another arrow.

And then the bough snapped.

For a second Corum seemed suspended in the air as he realised what had happened. There was a dull cracking noise,

77

a crash, and he was falling, trying futilely to grab at other branches as he went down, snow flying, making a terrible noise. The bow was wrenched from his hand; quiver and lances were still in the tree. He landed painfully on his left shoulder and thigh. If the snow had not been thick he would almost certainly have broken bones. As it was, the rest of his weapons were on the far side of the clearing and more of the Hounds of Kerenos were skulking in, having been momentarily surprised by the death of their brother and the sudden collapse of the tree branch.

Corum pulled himself to his feet and began to lope towards the bole against which his sword was leaning.

The horse whinnied and cantered towards him, blocking the path between him and his sword. Corum yelled at it, trying to force it out of the way. A long-drawn and triumphant howl came from behind him. Two huge paws struck his back and he went down. Hot, sticky saliva dripped on his neck. He tried to get up, but the giant dog pinned him, howling again to announce its victory. Corum had seen others of the hounds do the same thing. In a moment it would bare its fangs and rip his throat out.

But then Corum heard the horse's neighing, got an impression of flying hooves, and the dog's weight was off his body and he was rolling clear, seeing the great war-steed standing on its hind-legs and striking at the snarling hound with its iron-shod hooves. Half of the hound's head was caved in, but it still snapped at the horse. Then another hoof struck the skull and the dog collapsed with a groan.

Corum was already limping across the glade and then he had his silver hand on the scabbard, his fleshly hand on the hilt of the sword, and the blade was scraping free even as he turned back.

Tendrils of mist were sinuously entering the glade itself now, like searching, ghostly fingers. Already two more hounds were attacking the valiant war-horse which bled from two or three superficial bites but was still holding its own.

Then Corum saw a human figure appear from among the trees. Dressed all in leather, with a leather hood and heavy leather shoulder pads, it held a sword.

At first Corum thought that figure had come to aid him, for the face was as white as the bodies of the hounds and its eyes blazed red. He remembered the strange albino he had met at the Tower of Voilodion Ghagnasdiak. Was it Elric?

But no – the features were not the same. The features of this man were heavy, corrupt and his body was thick, unlike the slim form of Elric of Melniboné. He began to lumber knee-deep through the snow, the sword raised to deliver a blow.

Corum crouched and waited.

His opponent brought his sword down in a clumsy blow which Corum easily parried and returned, stabbing upward with all his strength to pierce the leather and drive the point of his blade into the man's heart. A peculiar grunt escaped the white-faced warrior's lips and he took three steps backward until the sword was free of his body. Then he took his own sword in both hands and swung it again at Corum.

Corum ducked barely in time. He was horrified. His thrust had been clean and true and the man had not died. He hacked at his opponent's exposed left arm, inflicting a deep cut. No blood spurted from the wound. The man seemed oblivious of it, slashing again at Corum.

Elsewhere in the darkness more of the hounds were bounding into the glade. Some merely sat on their haunches and watched the fight between the two men. Others set upon the war-horse whose own breath steamed in the cold night air. It was tiring now, the horse, and would soon be dragged down by the frightful dogs.

Corum stared in astonishment at his foe's pale face, wondering what manner of creature this actually was. Not Kerenos himself, surely? Kerenos had been described as a giant. No, this was one of the Fhoi Myore minions, of whom he had heard. A hound-master, perhaps, to Kerenos's hunt. The man had a small hunting dirk at his belt and the blade that he bore was not unlike a flenching cutlass used for stripping meat and hacking at the bones of large prey.

The man's eyes did not seem to focus on Corum at all, but on some distant goal. That was possibly why his responses were sluggish. Nonetheless, Corum was still winded from his fall and, if he could not kill his opponent, then sooner or later one of those clumsy blows would strike true and Corum would be slain.

Implacably, swinging the great cutlass from side to side, the white-faced warrior advanced on Corum who was barely able to do more than parry the blows.

He was retreating slowly backwards, knowing that behind him, at the edge of the glade, waited the hounds. And the hounds were panting – panting in hot-breathed anticipation, their tongues lolling, as ordinary domestic dogs might pant when they anticipated food.

Corum could think of no worse fate, at that moment, than to become meat for the Hounds of Kerenos. He tried to rally, to carry the attack to his enemy, and then his left heel struck a hidden tree-root, his ankle twisted, and he fell, hearing the note of a horn from the forest – a horn that could only belong to the one considered the greatest of the Fhoi Myore, Kerenos. Now the dogs were up, moving in on him as he tried to struggle up, his sword raised to ward off the blows which the white-faced warrior rained upon him.

Again the horn sounded.

The warrior paused, cutlass raised, a dull expression of puzzlement appearing on his heavy features. The dogs, too, were hesitating, red ears cocked, unsure of what they were expected to do.

And the horn sounded for the third time.

Reluctantly the hounds began to slink back into the forest. The warrior turned his back on Corum and staggered, dropping his blade, covering his ears, moaning softly, as he, too, followed the dogs from the glade. Then, suddenly, he stopped. His arms dropped limply to his sides, blood suddenly began to spurt from the wounds Corum had inflicted.

The warrior fell upon the snow and was still.

Warily, uncertainly, Corum got to his feet. His war-horse plodded up to him and nuzzled him. Corum felt a pang of guilt that he had considered leaving the brave beast to its fate when he had climbed the tree. He rubbed its nose. Though bleeding from several bites, the horse was not seriously hurt, and three of the devil dogs lay dead in the glade, their heads and bodies smashed by the horse's hooves.

A quietness fell upon the glade then. Corum used what he considered only a pause in the attack to seek his fallen bow. He found it, near the broken branch. But the arrows and his two lances remained where he had hung them in the tree. He stood on tiptoe, reaching up with his bow to try to dislodge them, but they were too high.

Then he heard a movement behind him and turned, sword at the ready.

A tall figure had entered the glade. He wore a long, pleated surcoat of soft leather, dyed a deep, rich blue. There were jewels on his slender fingers, a golden, jewelled collar at his throat and, beneath the surcoat, could just be seen a samite robe, embroidered with mysterious designs. The face was handsome and old, framed by long, grey hair and a grey beard that ended just above the golden collar. In one of his hands the newcomer held a horn – a long horn bound with bands of silver and gold, each band fashioned in the shape of a beast of the forest.

Corum drew himself up, dropping the bow and taking his sword in both hands.

'I face you, Kerenos,' said the Prince in the Scarlet Robe, 'and I defy you.'

The tall man smiled. 'Few have ever faced Kerenos.' His voice was mellow, weary and wise. 'Even I have not faced him.'

'You are not Kerenos? Yet you have his horn. You must have called off those hounds. Do you serve him?'

'I serve only myself – and those who aid me. I am Calatin. I was famous once, when there were folk in these parts to speak of me. I am a wizard. Once I had twenty-seven sons and a grandson. Now there is only Calatin.'

'There are many now who mourn sons – and daughters, too,' said Corum, recalling the old woman he had seen some days since.

'Many,' agreed the wizard Calatin. 'But my sons and my grandson died not in the battle against the Fhoi Myore. They

81

died on my behalf, seeking something I require in my own feud with the Cold Folk. But who are you, warrior, who fights the Hounds of Kerenos so well, and who sports a silver hand like the hand of some legendary demigod?'

'I am pleased that you, at least, do not recognise me,' said Corum. 'I am called Corum Jhaelen Irsei. The Vadhagh are my folk.'

'Sidhi folk, then?' The tall old man's eyes became reflective. 'What do you on the mainland?'

'I am upon a quest. I seek something for a people who dwell now at Caer Mahlod. They are my friends.'

'So Sidhi befriend mortals now. Perhaps there are some advantages to the Fhoi Myore's coming.'

'Of advantages and disadvantages I know nought,' said Corum. 'I thank you, wizard, for calling off those dogs.'

Calatin shrugged and tucked the horn away in the folds of his blue robe. 'If Kerenos himself had hunted with his pack, I should not have been able to aid you. Instead he sent one of those.' Calatin nodded towards the dead creature whom Corum had fought.

'And what are those?' Corum asked. He crossed the glade to look down at the corpse. It had stopped bleeding now, but the blood had congealed in all its wounds. 'Why could I not kill it with my blade while you could kill it by the blast of a horn?'

'The third blast always slays the Ghoolegh,' said Calatin with a shrug. 'If "slay" is the proper word to use, for the Ghoolegh folk are half-dead already. That is why you doubt-less found that one hard to slay. Normally they are bound to obey the first blast. A second blast will warn them and the third blast will kill them for failing to obey the first. They make good slaves, as a result. My horn-note, being subtly different to that of Kerenos's own horn, confused both dogs and Ghoolegh. But one thing the Ghoolegh knew – the third blast kills. So he died.'

'Who are the Ghoolegh?'

'The Fhoi Myore brought them with them from across the water to the east. They are a race bred to serve the Fhoi Myore.

I know little else about them.'

'Do you know from where the Fhoi Myore came originally?' asked Corum. He began to move around the camp, finding sticks to build up the fire he had extinguished. He noted that the mist had disappeared entirely now.

'No. I have ideas, of course.'

All the while he had spoken, Calatin had not moved but had watched Corum through narrowed eyes. 'I would have thought,' he continued, 'that a Sidhi would know more than a mere mortal wizard.'

'I do not know what the Sidhi folk are like,' Corum said. 'I am a Vadhagh – and not of your time. I come from another age, an earlier age, or even an age which does not exist, as such, in your universe. I know no more than that.'

'Why did you choose to come here?' Calatin seemed to accept Corum's explanation without surprise.

'I did not choose. I was summoned.'

'An incantation?' Now Calatin was surprised. 'You know a folk with power to summon the Sidhi to their aid? In Caer Mahlod? It is hard to believe.'

'In that,' Corum told him, 'I had some choice. Their incantation was weak. It could not have brought me to them against my will.'

'Ah,' Calatin seemed satisfied. Corum wondered whether the wizard had been displeased when he thought there were mortals more powerful at sorcery than himself. He looked hard into Calatin's face. There was something most enigmatic about the wizard's eyes. Corum was not sure that he trusted the man very much, for all Calatin had saved his life.

At last the fire began to blaze and Calatin moved towards it, extending his hands to warm them.

'What if the hounds attack again?' Corum asked.

'Kerenos is nowhere near. It will take him some days to discover what happened here and then we shall be gone, I hope.'

'You wish to accompany me?' Corum asked.

'I was going to offer you the hospitality of my lodgings,' said Calatin with a smile. 'They are not far from here.'

'Why were you wandering the forest at night?'

Calatin drew his blue robe about him and seated himself on cleared ground near the fire. The light from the blaze stained his face and beard red, giving him a somewhat demonic appearance. He raised his eyebrows at Corum's question.

'I was looking for you,' he said.

'Then you did know of my presence?'

'No. I saw smoke a day or so ago and I came to investigate it. I wondered what mortal could be daring the dangers of Laahr. Happily I got to you before the hounds could dine off your corpse. Without my horn, I could not, myself, have survived in these parts. Oh, and I have one or two other small sorceries to help me remain alive.' Calatin smiled a thin smile. 'It is the day of the sorcerer in this world, again. Once, only a few years since, I was deemed eccentric because of my interests. I was thought mad by some, evil by others. Calatin, they said, escapes from the real world by studying occult matters. What use can such things be to our people?' He chuckled. It was not entirely a pleasant sound to Corum's ears. 'Well, I have found some uses for the old lore. And Calatin is the only one to remain alive in the whole of the peninsula.'

'You have used your knowledge for selfish ends alone, it seems,' said Corum. He drew a skin of wine from his pack and offered it to Calatin, who accepted it without suspicion and who seemed to experience no rancour at Corum's remark. Calatin raised the skin to his lips and drank deeply before replying.

'I am Calatin,' said the wizard. 'I had a family. I have had several wives. I had twenty-seven sons and a grandson. They were all I could care for. And now that they are dead, I care for Calatin. Oh, do not judge me too harshly, Sidhi, for I was mocked by my fellows for many years. I divined something of the Fhoi Myore's coming, but they ignored me. I offered my help, but they laughed, they rejected it. I have no cause to love mortals much. But I have less cause to hate the Fhoi Myore, I suppose.'

'What became of your twenty-seven sons and your grandson?'

'They died together or individually in different parts of the world.'

'Why did they die if they did not fight the Fhoi Myore?'

'The Fhoi Myore killed some of them. They were all upon quests, seeking things I needed to continue my researches into certain aspects of mystic lore. One or two were succesful and, dying of their wounds, brought me those things. But there are still several things I need and, I suppose, shall not have, now.'

Corum made no response to Calatin's statement. He felt faint. As the fire warmed his blood and brought pain to the minor wounds he had sustained, he began to realise the full extent of his tiredness. His eyes began to close.

'You see,' Calatin continued, 'I have been frank with you, Sidhi. And what quest are you upon?'

Corum yawned. 'I seek a spear.'

In the dim firelight Corum thought he saw Calatin's eyes narrow.

'A spear?'

'Aye.' Corum yawned again and stretched his body beside the fire.

'And where do you seek this spear?'

'A place that some doubt exists, where the race I call Mabden – your race – does not dare go, or cannot go on pain of death, or . . .' Corum shrugged. 'It is hard to separate one superstition from another in this world of yours.'

'Is this place you go to – this place which might not exist – an island?'

'An island, aye.'

'Called Hy-Breasail?'

'That is its name.' Corum forced sleep away, becoming a little more alert. 'Do you know it?'

'I have heard it lies out to sea, to the west, and that the Fhoi Myore dare not visit it.'

'I have heard that, also. Do you know why the Fhoi Myore cannot go there?'

'Some say that the air of Hy-Breasail, while beneficial to mortals, is deadly to the Fhoi Myore. But it is not the air of the

85

island that endangers mortals – it is the enchantments of the place, they say, that bring death to ordinary men.'

'Enchantments . . . ?' Corum could resist sleep no longer.

'Aye,' echoed the wizard Calatin thoughtfully, 'enchantments of fearful beauty, it is said.'

They were the last words Corum heard before he fell into a deep and dreamless slumber.

6. OVER THE WATER TO HY-BREASAIL

In the morning Calatin led Corum from the forest and they stood beside the sea. Warm sun shone upon white beaches and blue water, yet behind them, still, the forest lay crushed by snow.

Corum was not riding his horse; he was reluctant to mount the brave beast until its wounds had healed, but he had gathered his gear, including his arrows and his lances, and laid it upon his mount's back where the load would not irritate the wounds it had sustained in the previous night's fight. Corum's own body was bruised and aching, but he forgot his discomfort as soon as he recognised the shore.

'So,' said Corum, 'I was merely a mile or two from the coast when those beasts attacked.' He smiled ironically. 'And there is Moidel's Mount.' He pointed along the shore to where the hill could be seen, rising from a deeper sea than when Corum had last visited it – but unmistakably the place where Rhalina's castle had stood, guarding the margravate of Lwym-an-Esh. 'Moidel's Mount remains.'

'I do not know the name you speak,' said Calatin, stroking his beard and arranging his finery as if about to receive a distinguished visitor, 'but my house is built upon that tor. It is where I have always lived.'

Corum accepted this and began to walk on towards the mount. 'I have lived there, too,' he said. 'And I was happy.'

Calatin, with long strides, caught up with him. 'You lived there, Sidhi? I know nothing of that.'

'It was before Lwym-an-Esh was drowned,' Corum explained. 'Before this cycle of history began. Mortals and gods come and go, but nature remains.'

'It is all relative,' Calatin said. Corum thought his tone a little peevish, as if he resented hearing this truism.

Nearing the place, Corum saw that once the old causeway had been replaced by a bridge, but now that bridge was in ruins, deliberately destroyed, it seemed. He commented on this to Calatin.

The wizard nodded. 'I destroyed the bridge. The Fhoi Myore and the things of the Fhoi Myore are, like the Sidhi, reluctant to cross western water.'

'Why western water?'

'I have no understanding of their customs. Have you any fear of wading through the shallows to the island, Sir Sidhi?'

'None,' said Corum. 'I have made the same journey many times. And do not draw too many conclusions from that, wizard, for I am not of the Sidhi race, though you seem to insist otherwise.'

'You spoke of Vadhagh and that is an old name for the Sidhi.'

'Perhaps legend has confused the two races.'

'You have the Sidhi look, nonetheless,' Calatin said flatly. 'The tide is retreating. Soon it will be possible to cross. We shall make our way along what remains of the bridge and enter the water from there.'

Corum continued to lead his horse, following Calatin as he set foot on the stone bridge and walked as far as he could until he reached crude steps which led down into the sea. 'It is shallow enough,' the wizard announced.

Corum looked at the green mount. There it was lush spring. He looked behind him. There it was cruel winter. How could nature be controlled so?

He had difficulty with the horse. Its hooves threatened to

slip on the wet rocks. But eventually both rider and horse were shoulder deep in the water and feeling with their feet for the remains of the old causeway below. Through the clear sea Corum could just make out the worn cobblestones that might have been the same ones he had stepped on a thousand or more years past. He remembered his first coming to Moidel's Mount. He remembered the hatred he had had, then, of all Mabden. And he had been betrayed by Mabden many times.

The wizard Calatin's cloak floated out behind him on the surface of the water as the tall old man led the way.

Slowly they began to emerge from the sea until they were two-thirds of the way across and the water was now only up to their shins. The horse snorted with pleasure. Evidently its soaking had soothed its wounds. It shook its mane and dilated its nostrils. Perhaps the sight of the good, green grass on the slopes of the tor also improved its spirits. Now there was no trace at all of Rhalina's castle. Instead, a villa had been built near the top – a villa two storeys high, made of white stone that sparkled in the sunshine. Its roof was of grey slate. A pleasant house, thought Corum, and not a typical one for a man who dabbled in the occult arts. He recalled his last sight of the old castle, burned by Glandyth in revenge.

Was that why he felt so suspicious of this Mabden, Calatin? Was there something of the Earl of Krae about him? Something in the eyes, the bearing, or, perhaps, the voice? It was foolish to make comparisons. Calatin did not have an agreeable manner, it was true, but it was possible that his motives were kindly. He had saved Corum's life, after all. It would not be fair to judge the wizard on his outward and seemingly very cynical comportment.

Now they began to climb the winding track to the top of the mount. Corum smelled the spring, the flowers and the rhododendrons, the grass and the budding trees. Sweet-scented moss covered the old rocks of the hill, birds nested in the larches and the alders and flew among the new, bright leaves. Corum had another reason now to be grateful to Calatin, for he had become profoundly weary of the deadness of the landscape.

And then they came to the house itself, Calatin showing Corum where he could stable his horse and then flinging open a door wide so that Corum could go first into the place. The ground floor consisted mainly of one large room whose wide windows were filled with glass and looked from one side to the open sea and from the other to the white and desolate land. Corum could observe how the clouds formed over the land but not over the sea. The clouds seemed to remain in one place, as if forbidden to cross an invisible barrier.

Corum had observed little glass in any other part of this Mabden world. Calatin had found benefits, it appeared, in his studying of ancient lore. The roofs of the house were high and supported by stone beams, and the rooms of the house, as Calatin showed it to him, were filled with scrolls, books, tablets and experimental apparatus; truly a wizard's lair.

Yet there was nothing sinister, to Corum, in Calatin's possessions or, indeed, his obsessions. The man called himself a wizard, but Corum would have called him a philosopher, someone who enjoyed exploring and discovering the secrets of nature.

'Here,' Calatin told him, 'I have almost everything saved from Lwym-an-Esh's libraries before that golden civilisation sank beneath the waves. Many mocked me and told me that I filled my head with nonsense, that my books were only the work of madmen who had preceded me and that they contained no more truth than my own work contained. They said that the histories were mere legends, that the grimoires were fantasies – fiction, that the talk of gods and demons and such was merely poetic, metaphorical. But I believed otherwise and I was proved correct.' Calatin smiled coldly. 'Their deaths proved me right.' The smile changed. 'Though I did not have very much satisfaction in knowing that all who might have apologised to me are now slain by the Hounds of Kerenos or frozen by the Fhoi Myore.'

'You have no pity for them, have you, wizard?' Corum said, seating himself upon a stool and staring through the window out to sea.

'Pity? No. It is not my character to know pity. Or guilt.

Or any of those other emotions which other mortals care so much for.'

'You do not feel guilty that you sent your twenty-seven sons and your grandson upon a fruitless series of quests?'

'They were not entirely fruitless. There is little more I seek now.'

'I meant that you must surely feel some remorse for the fact that they all died.'

'I do not know that all of them died. Some simply did not return. But, yes, most did die. It is a shame, I suppose. I would rather that they lived. But my interest is more in abstractions – pure knowledge – than the usual considerations which hold so many mortals in chains.'

Corum did not pursue the subject.

Calatin moved about the big room complaining of his wet clothes but making no effort to change them. They had dried before he next spoke to Corum.

'You go to Hy-Breasail, you said.'

'Aye. Do you know where the island lies?'

'If the island exists, yes. But all mortals who go close to the island, so it is said, are immediately put under a glamour – they see nothing, save perhaps a reef or cliffs impossible to scale. Only the Sidhi see Hy-Breasail as the island really looks. That, at least, is what I have read. None of my sons returned from Hy-Breasail.'

'They sought it and perished?'

'Losing several good boats into the bargain. Goffanon rules there, you see, and will have naught to do with mortals or Fhoi Myore. Some say he is the last of the Sidhi.' Calatin looked suddenly at Corum in suspicion. He drew back slightly. 'You are not . . . ?'

'I am Corum,' Corum said. 'I told you that. No, I am not Goffanon, but Goffanon (if he exists) is the one I seek.'

'Goffanon! He is powerful.' Calatin was frowning. 'But perhaps it is true and you are the only one who can find him. Perhaps we could make a bargain, Prince Corum.'

'If it is to our mutual benefit, aye.'

Calatin became pensive, fingering his beard, muttering to

himself. 'The only servants of the Fhoi Myore who do not fear the island and are not subject to its enchantments are the Hounds of Kerenos. Kerenos himself, even, fears Hy-Breasail – but not his hounds. Therefore you would be in danger, even there, of the dogs.' He looked up and looked hard at Corum. 'You might reach the island, but you probably would not live to find Goffanon.'

'If he exists.'

'Aye, aye – if he exists. I thought I guessed your quest when you spoke of the spear. That is Bryionak, I take it ?'

'Bryionak is its name.'

'One of the treasures of Caer Llud was it not ?'

'I believe that is common knowledge amongst your folk.'

'And why do you seek it ?'

'It will be useful to me against the Fhoi Myore. I can say no more.'

Calatin nodded. 'There is no more that needs saying. I will help you, Prince Corum. A boat? To go to Hy-Breasail? I have a boat you may borrow. And protection against the Hounds of Kerenos ? You may borrow my horn.'

'And what must I do in return ?'

'You must pledge me that you will bring me back something from Hy-Breasail. Something very valuable to me. Something which you can only get from the Sidhi smith Goffanon.'

'A jewel ? A charm ?'

'No. Much more.' Calatin fumbled among his papers and his equipment until he found a little bag of smooth, soft leather. 'This is watertight,' he said. 'You must use this.'

'What do you want ? Magic water from a well ?'

'No,' said Calatin urgently, quietly. 'You must bring me some of the spittle belonging to the Sidhi smith Goffanon. In this. Take it.' He reached inside his robes and drew out the beautiful horn he had used to drive away the Hounds of Kerenos. 'And take this. Blow it three times to drive them off. Blow it six times to set them upon an enemy.'

Corum fingered the ornate horn. 'It must be a powerful thing, indeed,' he murmured, 'if it can match that of Kerenos.'

'It was once a Sidhi horn,' Calatin told him.

* * *

92

An hour later Calatin had taken him to the far side of the mount where a little natural harbour still was. And in the harbour was a small sailing boat. Calatin gave Corum a chart and a lodestone. Corum carried the horn at his belt now and his own weapons were upon his back.

'Ah,' said the wizard Calatin, fingering his own noble skull with trembling fingers, 'perhaps at last I may have my ambition fulfilled. Do not fail, Prince Corum. For my sake, do not fail.'

'For the sake of the people of Caer Mahlod, for all the people who have not so far been slain by the Fhoi Myore, for the sake of a world in perpetual winter that might never see the spring again, I shall try not to fail, wizard.'

And then the sea-wind had caught the sail and the boat sped out over the sparkling water, heading west to where Lwym-an-Esh and her beautiful cities had once been.

And Corum fancied for a moment that he would find Lwym-an-Esh just as he had seen it last and that all the rest, all the events of the past weeks, would be a dream.

Moidel's Mount and the mainland were soon far behind, out of sight, and flat water lay all around him.

If Lwym-an-Esh had survived, he would have seen it by this time. But lovely Lwym-an-Esh was not there. The stories of her sinking beneath the waves were true. And would the stories be true of Hy-Breasail? Was it really all that was left of the land? And would he be subject to the same illusions suffered by previous voyagers?

He studied his charts. Soon he would know the answers. In another hour or so he would sight Hy-Breasail.

7. THE DWARF GOFFANON

Was this the beauty against which the old woman had warned him?

Certainly it was beguiling. It could only be the island named Hy-Breasail. It was not what he had thought he would find for all that it bore resemblance to parts of Lwym-an-Esh. The breeze caught the sail of his boat and blew him closer to the coast.

Surely there could be no danger here?

Soft seas whispered on the white beaches and the light wind stirred the green branches of cypress trees, willows, poplars, oaks and strawberry trees. Gentle, rolling hills protected quiet valleys. Flowering rhododendron bushes bloomed with deep scarlets, purples and yellows. Warm, glowing light touched the landscape and gave it a faint, golden haze.

Corum, as he looked upon the island, was filled with a deep sense of peace. He knew that he could rest there forever, be content to lie beside the sparkling, winding rivers, to walk over the sweet-smelling lawns looking at the deer, the squirrels and the birds which teemed there.

Another Corum, a young Corum, would have accepted this vision without question. After all, there had once been Vadhagh estates which resembled this island. But that had been the Vadhagh dream and the Vadhagh dream was over. Now he inhabited the Mabden dream – perhaps even the Fhoi Myore dream which was overwhelming it. Was there a place in either of those dreams for the land of Hy-Breasail?

So it was with a certain caution that Corum beached his boat upon the strand and then dragged it into the cover of some rhododendron bushes growing close to the shore. His weapons he adjusted in his harness so that they would be within easy reach and then he began to march inland, experiencing a certain guilt that so martial a figure as himself should be invading this peaceful place.

As he walked through groves and across meadows he passed small herds of deer which showed no fear of him and, indeed, other animals which showed open curiosity and came closer to investigate this stranger. It was possible, Corum thought, that he was under the spell of a powerful illusion, but it was hard to believe on anything but the most abstract of levels. Yet no Mabden had ever returned from the place and many voyagers denied finding it at all, while the Fhoi Myore, fearsome and cruel, were terrified of setting foot here, for all that legend said they had once conquered the whole land of which only this part remained. There were many mysteries, thought Corum, concerning Hy-Breasail, but there was no denying the fact that, to a weary mind and an exhausted body, there could be no more perfect a world.

He smiled as he saw the bright butterflies fluttering through the summer air, the peacocks and pheasants serene upon the green lawns. Even at its finest the landscape of Lwym-an-Esh could not have equalled this. Yet there was no sign of habitation. There were no ruins, no houses – not even a cave where a man might dwell. And perhaps that was what made him retain a shade of suspicion concerning this paradise. Yet one being, surely, did live here, and that was the smith Goffanon who protected his domain with enchantments and terrors which were said to bring death to any who dared invade it.

Subtle enchantments, indeed, thought Corum; and well-hidden terrors.

He paused to look at a small waterfall which flowed over limestone rocks. Rowan trees grew on the banks of the clear stream and in the stream were small trout and grayling. The sight of the fish, as well as the game he had seen earlier, began to make him feel hungry. He had eaten such poor fare since he had first gone to Caer Mahlod and he dearly wanted to unsling one of his lances and try to spear a fish. But something warned him against this action. It occurred to him – and it might have been a thought inspired by nothing more than superstition – that if he attacked even one of the denizens of the island then all the life of the island would turn against him. He determined to avoid killing as much as an irritating insect during his sojourn on Hy-Breasail and took, instead, a piece of dried meat from his pouch and began to gnaw on that as he walked. He was climbing uphill now, towards a great boulder which seemed perched on the very top of the slope.

The climb became steeper the nearer to the top he came, but at last he reached the boulder and paused, leaning against it and looking about him. He had expected to see the whole of the island from this eminence, for it was certainly the highest hill he had seen. But, strangely, he saw no sea at all in any direction.

A peculiar shimmering mist, blue and flecked with gold, was on every horizon. It seemed to Corum to follow, perhaps, the coastline of the island, for it was irregular. Yet why had he not seen it when he first landed? Was it this mist which kept the eyes of most travellers from sight of Hy-Breasail?

He shrugged. The day was warm and he was tired. He found a smaller rock in the shade of the great boulder and sat down on it, drawing a small flask of wine from his pouch and sipping it slowly as he let his gaze wander over the valleys, groves and streams of the island. Everywhere it was the same, as if carefully landscaped by a gardener of genius. He had already come to the conclusion that Hy-Breasail's countryside was not wholly natural in origin. It was more like a great park, such as the Vadhagh had created at the height of their culture. Perhaps that was why the animals were so tame, he thought. It could be that they all led protected lives and so trusted mortals like himself, having had no experience of danger at the hands of two-legged creatures. Yet he was again forced to remind himself of the Mabden who had not returned, of the Fhoi Myore who had conquered the place and then fled, fearing ever to return.

He felt drowsy. He yawned and stretched himself out on the grass. His eyes closed and his mind began to wander a little as sleep slowly overwhelmed him.

And he dreamed that he spoke to a youth whose flesh was all gold and from whom, in some odd way, a great harp grew. And the youth, who smiled without kindness, began to play upon his harp. And Medhbh the warrior princess listened to the music and her face became full of hatred for Corum and she found a shadowy figure who was Corum's enemy and directed him to slay Corum.

And Corum woke up, still hearing the strange music of the harp. But the music faded before he could determine whether he had actually heard it or whether it had lingered on from his dream.

The nightmare had been a cruel one and it had made him afraid. He had never dreamed such a dream before. It was possible, he thought, that he was beginning to understand something of the peculiar dangers of this island. Perhaps it was in the nature of the island to turn men's minds in on themselves and let them create their own terrors – terrors far worse than any others which might be inflicted upon them. He would avoid sleep, if he could, from now on.

And then he wondered if he were not still dreaming, for there came in the distance the familiar sound of the baying of hounds, the Hounds of Kerenos. Had they followed him to the island, swimming across a score of miles of sea? Or had they come already to Hy-Breasail, to wait for him? He touched the ornate horn at his belt as their yapping and howling came closer. He scanned the land for sight of them, but all he could see was a startled herd of deer led by a great stag bounding across a meadow and into a forest. Did the hounds pursue the herd? No. The hounds did not appear.

He saw something else moving in a valley on the other side

of the hill. He guessed that it was probably another deer, but then he realised that it ran on two legs in peculiar leaping bounds. It was heavy, tall, and it carried something which flashed whenever the sun's rays touched it. A man?

Corum saw a white hide in the trees some distance behind the man. Then he saw another. Then there burst from the grove a pack of some twelve great dogs with tufted, red-tipped ears. The hounds pursued what was for them more familiar quarry than deer.

The man – if man it was – began to leap up a rocky hillside, following the course of a big waterfall, but this did not deter the dogs who kept implacably upon his track. The hillside became almost sheer, but still the man climbed – and still the dogs followed. Corum was amazed at their agility. Again something bright flashed. Corum realised that the man had turned and that the bright thing was a weapon which he was wielding to ward off the attack. It was obvious to Corum that the dogs' victim would not last for long.

It was only then that he remembered the horn. Hastily he raised it to his lips and blew three long blasts in quick succession. The notes of the horn sounded out clear and sharp across the valley. The dogs turned and began to circle, as if scenting, though their quarry was in easy sight.

Then the Hounds of Kerenos began to lope away. Corum laughed in delight. For the first time he had won a victory over the hellish dogs.

At his laughter, it seemed, the man on the far side of the valley looked up. Corum waved to him but the man did not return the wave.

As soon as the Hounds of Kerenos had disappeared, Corum began to run down the hillside towards the one whom he had helped. It did not take him long to reach the bottom of the slope and begin to ascend the next. He recognised the waterfall and the shelf of rock where the man had turned to do battle with the hounds, but the man himself was nowhere to be seen. He had not climbed higher, that was certain, neither had he come down, Corum was sure, for he had had a fairly clear view of the waterfall as he ran.

'Ho, there!' shouted the Prince in the Scarlet Robe, brandishing his horn. 'Where are you hiding, comrade?'

He was answered only by the rattling of water upon rocks as the waterfall continued its progress down the cliff face. He stared about him, peering at every shadow, every rock and bush, but it was as if the man had actually become invisible.

'Where are you, stranger?'

There was a faint echo, but this was drowned quickly by the sound of the water hissing and slapping as it foamed over the crags.

Corum shrugged and turned away, thinking it ironic that the men should be more timid than the beasts on the island.

And then suddenly, from nowhere, he felt a heavy blow in the small of his back and he was tumbling forward on to the heather, arms outstretched to break his fall.

'Stranger, eh?' said a deep surly voice. 'Call me stranger, eh?'

Corum struck the ground and rolled over, trying to free his sword from its scabbard.

The man who had pushed him was massive. He must have stood eight feet high and was a good four feet broad at the shoulder. He wore a polished iron breastplate, polished iron greaves, inlaid with red gold, and an iron helm upon his shaggy, black-bearded head. In his monstrous hands was the largest war-axe Corum had ever seen.

Corum scrambled up, drawing his blade. He suspected that this was the one whom he had saved. But the huge creature appeared to feel no gratitude at all.

Corum managed to gasp: 'Whom do I fight?'

'You fight me. You fight the Dwarf Goffanon,' said the giant.

8. THE SPEAR BRYIONAK

In spite of his danger, Corum found himself grinning in disbelief. 'Dwarf?'

The Sidhi smith glared at him.

'Aye? What is funny?'

'I should be afraid to meet ordinary-sized men on this island!'

'I miss your point.' Goffanon's eyes narrowed as he readied his axe and took up a fighting stance.

It was only then that Corum realised that the eyes were the same as his own remaining single orb – almond-shaped, yellow and purple – and that the self-called dwarf's skull structure was more delicate than it had at first appeared due to the beard covering so much of it. His face was, in most particulars, a Vadhagh face. Yet in all other respects Goffanon did not resemble a member of Corum's own race.

'Are there others of your kind in Hy-Breasail?' Corum used the pure tongue of the Vadhagh, not the dialect spoken by most Mabden, and produced an expression of gaping-mouthed astonishment on Goffanon's features.

'I am the only one,' the smith replied in the same tongue. 'Or thought so. Yet if you be of my folk, why did you set your dogs upon me?'

'They are not my dogs. I am Corum Jhaelen Irsei, of the Vadhagh race.' With his left hand, his silver hand, Corum held up the horn. 'This is what controls the dogs. This horn. They think their master sounds it.'

Goffanon lowered his axe a fraction. 'So you are not some servant of the Fhoi Myore?'

'I hope that I am not. I battle the Fhoi Myore and all that they stand for. Those dogs have attacked me more than once. It was to save me from further attacks that I was loaned the horn by a Mabden wizard.' Corum decided that this was a judicious time to sheathe his sword and hope that the Sidhi smith did not take the opportunity to split his skull.

Goffanon frowned, sucking at his lips as he debated Corum's words.

'How long have the Hounds of Kerenos been on your island?' Corum asked.

'This time? A day – no more. But they have been before. They seem the only things unaffected by the madness which comes upon the rest of the denizens of this world when they set foot upon my shores. And since the Fhoi Myore have had an abiding hatred for Hy-Breasail, they do not rest in sending their minions to hunt me. Often I am able to anticipate their coming and take precautions, but this time I had grown too confident, not expecting them back so soon. I thought you to be some new creature, some huntsman like the Ghoolegh (of whom I have heard) who serve Kerenos. But it seems to me now that I once listened to a tale concerning a Vadhagh with a strange hand and only one eye, but that Vadhagh died, even before the Sidhi came.'

'You do not call yourself Vadhagh?'

'Sidhi, we are called.' Now Goffanon had lowered his axe completely. 'We are related to your folk. Some of your people visited us once, I know – and we visited you. But that was when access to the fifteen planes was possible, before the last Conjunction of the Million Spheres.'

'You are from another plane. Then how did you reach this one?'

'A disruption in the walls between the realms. Thus came

the Fhoi Myore, from the Cold Places, from Limbo. And thus we came – to help the folk of Lwym-an-Esh and their Vadhagh friends – and fought the Fhoi Myore. There was great slaying in those days, long ago, and huge wars, which sank Lwym-an-Esh, killing all the Vadhagh and most of the Mabden – also my folk, the Sidhi, were slain, for we could not return to our own plane, since the rupture swiftly mended. We thought all the Fhoi Myore destroyed, but lately they have returned.'

'And you do not fight them?'

'I am not strong enough, alone. This island is physically part of my own plane. Here I can live in peace, save for the dogs. I am old, I shall die in a few hundred years.'

'I am weak,' Corum said. 'Yet I fight the Fhoi Myore.'

Goffanon nodded. Then he shrugged. 'Only because you have not fought them before,' he said.

'Yet why can they not come to Hy-Breasail? Why do no Mabden return from the island?'

'I try to keep the Mabden away,' said Goffanon, 'but they are an intrepid little race. Their very courage brings about their dreadful deaths. But I will tell you more when we have eaten. Will you guest with me, cousin?'

'Gladly,' said Corum.

'Then come.'

Goffanon began to climb back up the rocks, worked his way around the ledge on which he had stood to fight the Hounds of Kerenos, and disappeared again. His head reappeared again almost instantly. 'This way. I have lived here since the dogs began to plague me.'

Corum climbed slowly after the Sidhi, reached the ledge and saw that it went around a slab of rock which hid an entrance to a cave. The slab could be moved in grooves to block the entrance and, as Corum stepped through, Goffanon put his gigantic shoulder to the slab and heaved it into place. Inside was light coming from well-made lamps set in niches in the walls. The furniture was plain but expertly carved and there were woven tapestries upon the floor. Save for the lack of a window, Goffanon's lair was more than comfortable.

While Corum rested in a chair Goffanon busied himself at

his stove, preparing soup, vegetables and meat. The smell that arose from his pots was delicious and Corum congratulated himself for curbing his desire to spear fish from the stream. This meal promised to be much more appetising.

Goffanon, apologising for the scarcity of his plate, for he had lived alone for hundreds of years, put a huge bowl of soup before Corum. The Vadhagh prince ate gratefully.

Next followed meat and a variety of succulent vegetables which were, in turn, followed by the best-tasting fruit Corum had ever eaten. When, at last, he sank back in his chair it was with a feeling of well-being such as he had not experienced in years. He thanked Goffanon profusely and the self-styled dwarf's huge frame seemed to writhe in embarrassment. He apologised again and then seated himself in his own chair and put an object into his mouth which was like a small cup from which projected a long stalk which Goffanon sucked at, holding over the bowl of the little cup a piece of burning wood. Soon clouds of smoke issued from the bowl and from his mouth and he smiled with contentment, only noticing Corum's surprised expression sometime later. 'A custom of my folk,' he explained. 'It is an aromatic herb which we burn in this way and inhale the smoke. It pleases us.'

The smoke did not smell particularly sweet to Corum, but he accepted the Sidhi's explanation, though he refused Goffanon's offer of a bowl of his own smoke.

'You asked,' said Goffanon slowly, half-closing his huge, almond-shaped eyes, 'why the Fhoi Myore feared this island and why the Mabden perished here. Well, neither is any deliberate doing of mine, though I am glad that the Fhoi Myore avoided me. Long ago, during the period of the first Fhoi Myore invasion, when we were called to help our Vadhagh cousins and their friends, we had great difficulty in breaching the wall between the realms. Finally we did so, causing enormous disruptions in the world of our own plane, resulting in a great piece of land coming with us through the dimensions to your world. That piece of land settled, luckily, upon a relatively unpopulated part of the kingdom of Lwym-an-Esh. However, it retained the properties of our plane – it is, as it were, part of the Sidhi dream, rather than the Vadhagh, the Mabden or the Fhoi Myore dreams; though, as you will have noted, of course, the Vadhagh being closely related to the Sidhi have little difficulty in adapting themselves to it. The Mabden and the Fhoi Myore, on the other hand, cannot survive here at all. Madness overwhelms them as soon as they land. They enter a world of nightmare. All their fears multiply and become completely real for them and they are thus destroyed by their own terrors.'

'I guessed something of this,' Corum told Goffanon. 'For I had a hint of what might happen when I slept earlier today.'

'Exactly. Even the Vadhagh sometimes experienced a little of what it means for a mortal Mabden to land on Hy-Breasail. I try to hide the island's outlines with a mist I am able to prepare, but it is not always possible to keep a sufficient supply of the mist in the air. That is when the Mabden find the island and suffer enormously as a result.'

'And where do the Fhoi Myore originate from? You spoke of the Cold Places.'

'The Cold Places, aye. Do you not know of them in Vadhagh lore? The places *between* the planes – a chaotic limbo which occasionally spawns intelligence of sorts. That is what the Fhoi Myore are – creatures from Limbo who fell through the breach in the wall between the realms and arrived upon this plane, whereupon they embarked upon conquest of your world, planning to turn it into another limbo where they might best survive. They cannot live for much longer, the Fhoi Myore. Their own diseases destroy them. But they will live long enough, I fear, to bring freezing death to all but Hy-Breasail, to bring freezing death to Mabden and to all beasts, even the smallest sea-creature, on this world. It is inevitable. They will probably outlive me, some of them – Kerenos, anyway – but their plagues will slay them at last. Virtually all this world, save the land from which you have just come, has died under their rule. It happened quickly, I think. We thought them all dead, but they must have found hiding places – perhaps at the edge of the world where ice always may be found. Now their patience is rewarded, eh?' Goffanon sighed. 'Well,

well – there are other worlds – and those they cannot reach.'

'I wish to save this one,' said Corum quietly. 'I would save what is left, at least. I am sworn to that. Sworn to help the Mabden. Now I quest for their lost treasures. It was rumoured that you have one of those, something you made for the Mabden in their first fight with the Fhoi Myore, ages since.'

Goffanon nodded. 'You speak of the spear called Bryionak. I made it. Here it is only an ordinary spear, but in the Mabden dream and the Fhoi Myore dream it has great power.'

'So I heard.'

'It will tame, among other things, the Bull of Crinanass, which we brought with us when we came.'

'A Sidhi beast?'

'Aye. One of a great herd. He is the last.'

'Why did you seek the spear and carry it back to Hy-Breasail?'

'I have not left Hy-Breasail. That spear was brought by one of the mortals who came exploring. I tried to comfort him as he died raving, but he could not be comforted. When he had died I took my spear. That is all. He had thought, it seemed, that Bryionak would protect him from the dangers of my island.'

'So you would not deny the Mabden its help again.'

Goffanon frowned. 'I do not know. I am fond of that spear. I should not like to lose it again. And it will not help the Mabden much, cousin. They are doomed. It is best to accept that. They are doomed. Why not let them die swiftly? To send them Bryionak would be to offer them a false hope.'

'It is in my nature to put my faith in hopes, no matter how false they seem,' Corum said quietly.

Goffanon looked at him sympathetically. 'Aye. I was told of Corum. Now I recall the tale. You are a sad one. A noble one. But what happens, happens. There is nothing you can do to stop it.'

'I must try, you see, Goffanon.'

'Aye.' Goffanon pulled his great bulk from the chair and went to one side of the cave which was in shadow.

He returned bearing a spear of very ordinary appearance. It had a well-worn wooden shaft, was bound in iron. Only its head had something odd about its manufacture. Like the blade of Goffanon's axe, it shone brighter than ordinary iron.

The Sidhi handled it with pride. 'My tribe was always the smallest of the Sidhi, both in numbers and in stature, but we had our skills. We could work metals in a way which you might describe as philosophical. We understood that metals had qualities beyond their obvious properties. And so we made weapons for the Mabden. We made several. Of them all, only this survives. I made it. The spear Bryionak.'

He held it out to Corum who, for some reason, accepted it with his left hand, the silver hand. It was beautifully weighted, a practical weapon of war, but, if Corum had expected to sense in it anything extraordinary, he was disappointed.

'A good, plain spear,' said Goffanon, 'Bryionak.'

Corum nodded. 'Save for the head, that is.'

'No more of that metal can be smelted,' Goffanon told him. 'A little of it came with us when we left our own plane. A few axe blades, a sword or two – and that spear – were all we could manufacture. Good, sharp metal. It does not dull or rust.'

'And it has magical properties?'

Goffanon laughed. 'Not to the Sidhi. But the Fhoi Myore think so. As do the Mabden. Therefore, of course, it has magical properties. Spectacular properties. Yes, I am glad to have my spear back.'

'You would not part with it again?'

'I think not.'

'But the Bull of Crinanass will obey the one who wields it. And the Bull will aid the people of Caer Mahlod against the Fhoi Myore – perhaps help them destroy the Fhoi Myore.'

'Neither bull nor spear is powerful enough to do that,' said Goffanon gravely. 'I know that you want the spear, Corum, but I repeat this – nothing can save the Mabden world. It is doomed to die, just as the Fhoi Myore are doomed, just as I am doomed – and you also, unless you have a means of returning to your own plane (for I take it you are not from this one).'

'I am doomed, too, I think,' said Corum quietly. 'But I would carry the spear Bryionak back to Caer Mahlod, for that was my oath, that is my quest.'

Goffanon sighed and took the spear from Corum's hand. 'No,' he said. 'When the Hounds of Kerenos come again I shall need all my weapons to destroy them. The pack which attacked me today is doubtless still upon the island. If I kill that pack there will come another pack. My spear and my axe, they are my only security. You have yon horn, after all.'

'It is only loaned to me.'

'By whom?'

'By a wizard. Calatin's his name.'

'Aha. I tried to turn three of his sons away from this shore. But they died, as the others died.'

'I know that many of his sons came here.'

'What did they seek?'

Corum laughed. 'They wanted you to spit upon them.' He recalled the little watertight bag Calatin had given him. He drew it from his pouch.

Goffanon frowned. Then his brow cleared and he shook his head, puffing at the little bowl of herbs which still burned near his mouth. Corum wondered where he had witnessed a similar custom, but his memory had become very hazy, of late, concerning his previous adventures. That was the price one paid, he guessed, for entering another dream, another plane.

Goffanon sniffed. 'Another of their superstitions, no doubt. What do they do with these things? Animals' blood drawn at midnight. Bones. Roots. How debased has Mabden knowledge become!'

'Would you grant the wizard his wish?' Corum asked. 'I am pledged to ask you. He loaned me the horn on that understanding.'

Goffanon stroked his heavy beard. 'It has come to something when the Vadhagh must beg the Mabden for their help.'

'This is a Mabden world,' Corum said. 'You made that point yourself, Goffanon.'

'A Fhoi Myore world soon. And then no world at all. Ah, well, if it will help you, I will do what you want. I can lose nothing by it and I doubt if your wizard will gain anything, either. Hand me the bag.'

Corum passed the bag to Goffanon who grunted, laughed again, shook his head again, and spat into the bag, handing it back to Corum who, somewhat fastidiously, replaced it in his pouch.

'But it was the spear I really sought,' said Corum quietly. He regretted his insistence, after Goffanon had taken his other request with such good humour and, as well, had offered him good hospitality.

'I know.' Goffanon lowered his head and stared at the floor. 'But if I help you save a few Mabden lives, I stand the chance of losing my own.'

'Have you forgotten the generosity which led you and your people to come here in the first place?'

'I was more generous in those days. Besides, it was our kin, the Vadhagh, who asked for that help.'

'I am your kin, then,' Corum pointed out. He felt a pang of guilt at playing on the Sidhi dwarf's better feelings. 'And I ask.'

'One Sidhi, one Vadhagh, seven Fhoi Myore and still a fair horde of the ever-breeding Mabden. Yet it is not much compared with what I saw when first I came to this world. And the land was lovely. It bloomed. Now it is harsh and nothing will grow. Let it die, Corum. Stay with me here in the fair island, in Hy-Breasail.'

'I made a bargain,' said Corum simply. 'Everything in me would force me to agree with you and to accept your offer, Goffanon – save for that one thing. I made a bargain.'

'But my bargain – the bargain the Sidhi made – that is over. And I owe you nothing, Corum.'

'I helped you when the devil dogs attacked you.'

'I helped you keep your bargain with the Mabden wizard. Have I not paid that debt?'

'Must all things be discussed in terms of bargains, of debts?'

'Yes,' said Goffanon seriously, 'for it is nearly the end of the world and there are only a few things left in the world. They must be bartered and a balance kept. I believe that, Corum. It is not an attitude inspired by venality – we Sidhi were rarely considered venal – but by a necessary conception of order. What have you to offer me more useful to me in so many ways than the spear Bryionak?'

'Nothing, I think.'

'Only the horn. The horn that will dismiss the dogs when they attack me. That horn is more valuable to me than the spear. And the spear – is that not more valuable to you than the horn?'

'I agree,' said Corum. 'But the horn is not mine, Goffanon. The horn is only lent to me – by Calatin.'

'I will not give you Bryionak,' Goffanon said heavily, almost reluctantly, 'unless you give me the horn. That is the only bargain I will strike with you, Vadhagh.'

'And it is the only one I have no right to make.'

'Is there nothing Calatin wants from you?'

'I have already made my bargain with Calatin.'

'You cannot make another.'

Corum drew his brows together and with his right hand he fingered his embroidered eye-patch, as he was wont to do when faced with a difficult problem. He owed Calatin his life. Calatin would owe Corum nothing until Corum returned from the island with the little bag of the Sidhi's spittle. Then neither would be in the other's debt.

Yet the spear was important. Even now Caer Mahlod might be under attack from the Fhoi Myore and the only thing which might save them would be the spear Bryionak and the Bull of Crinanass. And Corum had sworn that he would return with the spear. He plucked the horn from where it hung at his hip by the long thong looped over his shoulder. He looked at the fine, mottled bone, the ornamental bands, the silver mouth-piece. It was a hero's horn. Who had borne it before Calatin found it? Kerenos himself?

'I could blow this horn now and bring the dogs upon us both,' Corum said musingly. 'I could threaten you, Goffanon, and make you give me Bryionak in return for your life.'

'Would you do that, cousin?'

'No.' Corum let the horn fall. Then, without realising that he had made a decision before he spoke, he said:

'Very well, Goffanon. I will give you the horn for the spear and try to make some other bargain with Calatin when I return to the mainland.'

'It is a sad bargain that we make,' said Goffanon, handing him the spear. 'Has it harmed our friendship?'

'I think that it has,' said Corum. 'I shall leave now, Goffanon.'

'You think me ungenerous?'

'No. I feel no rancour. I feel merely sad that we are all brought to this, that our nobility is somehow warped by our circumstances. You lose more than a spear, Goffanon. And I too lose something.'

Goffanon let out a mighty sigh. Corum gave him the horn that was not Corum's to give.

'I fear the consequences of this,' Corum said. 'I suspect that I shall face more than a Mabden wizard's wrath by giving you the horn.'

'Shadows fall across the world,' said Goffanon. 'And many strange things can hide in those shadows. Many things can be born, unseen and unsuspected. These are days for fearing shadows, Corum Jhaelen Irsei, and we should be fools if we did not fear them. Yes, we are brought low. Our pride diminishes. May I walk with you to the shore?'

'To the borders of your sanctuary? Why not come with me, Goffanon, to fight – to wield that great axe of yours against our foes? Would such an action not restore your pride?'

'I think not,' said Goffanon sadly. 'A little of the cold has come to Hy-Breasail, too, you see.'

Book Three

More bargains made while the
Fhoi Myore march

1. WHAT THE WIZARD
DEMANDED

As Corum beached the boat in the small bay of Moidel's Mount he heard footsteps behind him. He turned, reaching for his sword. The transition from the peace and beauty of Hy-Breasail to the outside world had brought with it depression and a certain amount of fear. Moidel's Mount, which had seemed such a welcome sight when he had first seen it again, now looked faded and sinister and he wondered if the Fhoi Myore dream had begun to touch the tor at last or whether the place had merely seemed pleasanter in comparison with the dark and frozen forest in which he had originally met the wizard.

Calatin stood there, tall in his blue robe, white-haired and handsome. There was a hint of anxiety in his eyes.

'Did you find the Glamorous Isle?'

'I found it.'

'And the Sidhi smith?'

Corum picked the spear Bryionak from out of the boat. He showed it to Calatin.

'But what of my request?' Calatin seemed hardly interested at all in a spear which was one of the treasures of Caer Llud, a mystic weapon of legend.

Corum found it faintly amusing that Calatin should care so

little for Bryionak and so much about a little sack of saliva. He drew the pouch out and handed it to the wizard who sighed with relief and grinned with pleasure.

'I am grateful to you, Corum. And I am glad that I was able to serve you. Did you encounter the hounds?'

'Once,' said Corum.

'The horn aided you?'

'It aided me. Aye.' Corum began to walk up the beach, Calatin following.

They reached the brow of the hill and looked towards the mainland where the world was cold and white and brooding grey cloud filled the sky.

'Will you stay the night with me?' Calatin said. 'And tell me of Hy-Breasail and what you discovered there?'

'No,' said Corum. 'Time grows short and I must ride back for Caer Mahlod, for I feel that the Fhoi Myore will attack that place. They must know, by now, that I aid their enemies.'

'It is likely. You will want your horse.'

'Aye,' said Corum.

There was a pause. Calatin began to say something and then changed his mind. He led Corum to the stable below the house and there was the war-horse, almost healed from its wounds. It snorted in recognition when it saw Corum. Corum stroked its nose and led it from the stable.

'My horn,' said Calatin. 'Where is that?'

'I left it,' Corum told him, 'in Hy-Breasail.' He looked directly into the wizard's eyes and saw those eyes heat with fear and anger.

'How?' Calatin almost screamed. 'How could you mislay it?'

'I did not mislay it.'

'You left it there deliberately? It was agreed that you should borrow it. That was all.'

'I gave it to Goffanon. In a way you could say that if I had not had the horn to give him I could not have got you what you want.'

'Goffanon? Goffanon has my horn?' Calatin's eyes became colder. They narrowed.

'Aye.'

There was no excuse Corum could make, so he said nothing further. He waited for Calatin to speak.

Then the wizard said:

'You are in my debt again, Vadhagh.'

'Aye.'

The wizard's tone was level now, calculating. He smiled a quiet, unpleasant smile. 'You must give me something to replace my horn.

'What do you want?' Corum was becoming tired of bargaining. He was anxious to ride away from Moidel's Mount, to return as swiftly as possible to Caer Mahlod.

'I must have something,' said Calatin. 'You understand that, I trust?'

'Tell me what, wizard.'

Calatin looked Corum over as a farmer might look over a horse at market. Then he reached out and touched the surcoat Corum wore beneath the fur cloak the Mabden had given him. It was Corum's Vadhagh robe, red and light and made from the delicate skin of a beast which had dwelt once upon another plane and which had become extinct even there.

'Your robe, prince, is of great value, I think?'

'I have never considered its price. It is my Name-robe. Every Vadhagh has one.'

'Then is it not valuable to you?'

'Is this what you want, my robe? Will that satisfy you for the loss of the horn?' Corum spoke impatiently. His liking for the wizard had not increased. Yet he was morally in the wrong, he knew. And Calatin knew that, too.

'If you think it a fair bargain?'

Corum flung off the fur robe and began to unbuckle his belt, to undo the pin which attached his robe to his shoulder. It would be strange to lose the garment he had worn for so long, but he attached no special sentiment to it. The other robe warmed him well enough. He did not need his scarlet one.

He handed the robe to Calatin. 'There you are, wizard. Now we are neither of us in the other's debt.'

'Just so,' said Calatin, watching as Corum buckled on his

weapons and then climbed into the high saddle of the horse. 'I wish you a good journey, Prince Corum. And be wary of the Hounds of Kerenos. After all, there is no horn to save you now.'

'And none to save you,' said Corum. 'Will they attack you?'

'It is unlikely.' Calatin spoke mysteriously. 'It is unlikely.'

And then Corum rode down to the drowned causeway and entered the sea.

He did not look back at the wizard Calatin. He looked ahead, at the snow-buried land, not relishing the prospect of his journey back to Caer Mahlod, but glad to be leaving Moidel's Mount. He clutched the spear Bryionak in his silver hand, his left hand, and he guided his horse with his right, and soon he had reached the mainland and his breath and the breath of his horse began to steam in the chill air. He headed north-west.

And, as he entered the bleak forest, he thought for a moment that he heard the sound of a wild and melancholy harp.

2. THE FHOI MYORE MARCH

The horseman rode a beast that was only a little like a horse. Both were coloured a strange, pale green. There were no shades of colour in either. The snow was churned by the beast's hooves. The snow flew high on both sides of it. The horseman's pale green face was blank, as if the snow had frozen it. His pale green eyes were cool. And in his hand was a pale green sword. Not too far distant from Corum, who was drawing his own blade, the rider came to a sudden halt, crying out:

'Are you the one they think will save them? You seem more man than god to me!'

'Man I am,' said Corum evenly. 'And warrior. Do you challenge me?'

'Balahr challenges you. I am merely his instrument.'

'Balahr does not wish to fight me himself, then?'

'The Fhoi Myore do not fight hand to hand with mortals. Why should they?'

'The Fhoi Myore have much fear in them for a race so powerful. What is the matter with them? Do the diseases which eat at them, which will at last destroy them, weaken them?'

'I am Hew Argech, lately of the White Rocks, beyond Karnec. There was once a people, an army, a tribe. Now there is me. And I serve Balahr the One-eyed. What else can I do?'

'Serve your own folk, the Mabden.'

'The trees are my folk. The pines. They keep us both alive, my steed and me. The sap in my veins is nurtured not by meat and drink but by earth and rain. I am Hew Argech, brother to the pines.'

Corum could hardly believe the import of what this creature said. A man he must have been once, but now he had changed – been changed by Fhoi Myore sorcery. Corum's respect for Fhoi Myore power increased.

'Will you dismount, Hew Argech, and fight a manly fight, sword against sword in the snow?' Corum asked.

'I cannot. Once I fought so,' The voice was innocent, like the voice of a candid child. But the eyes remained blank, the face expressionless. 'Now I must fight with cunning, not honour.'

And Hew Argech was charging forward again, sword whirling as he bore down on Corum.

It had been a week since Corum had left Moidel's Mount; a week of bitter cold. His bones were stiff with it. His eye had blurred from looking at nothing but snow, so that it had been some time before he had seen the pale green rider on the pale green steed come riding across the white moor.

So quick was Hew Argech's attack that Corum barely had time to bring his own sword up to block the first blow. Then Hew Argech had passed him and was turning his beast for a second assault. This time Corum charged and his sword nicked Hew Argech's arm, but Argech's sword clanged on Corum's breastplate and half-knocked the Vadhagh prince from his saddle. Corum still clutched the spear Bryionak in his silver hand, and the silver hand also gripped the reins of his snorting war-horse as it lumbered round, up to its knees in thick snow, to face the next attack.

The two fought in this manner for some time, with neither managing to break the other's guard. Corum's breath issued from his mouth in great clouds, but no breath at all seemed to escape Hew Argech's lips and the pale green man showed no signs of tiring, while Corum was desperately weary, barely able to keep a grip on his sword.

It was obvious to Corum that Hew Argech knew he was tiring and was merely waiting until he should become so dazed that a quick sword-thrust would finish him. Several times he managed to rally himself, but now Argech was circling him, thrusting, slicing, battering, and then his sword was knocked from his frozen fingers and there came from Hew Argech's mouth a peculiar, rustling laugh, like wind through leaves, and he bore down on Corum for the last time.

Swaying in his saddle, Corum brought up the spear Bryionak to defend himself and managed to block the next blow. As Hew Argech's sword struck the head of the spear it clanged with a musical, silvery note, which surprised both opponents. Argech had gone past Corum again, but was turning rapidly. Corum flung back his left arm and threw the spear with such force at the pale green warrior he fell forward over his horse's neck and had strength enough only to raise his head to see the Sidhi spear pierce Hew Argech's chest.

Hew Argech sighed and he fell from the back of his pale green beast, the spear protruding from him.

Then Corum saw something that amazed him. How it happened he could not be sure, but the spear left the body of the pale green man and flew back into the open palm of Corum's silver hand. The hand closed involuntarily around the shaft.

Corum blinked his eye, barely able to believe what had happened, though he could feel, as well as see, the spear, for its shaft rested partly against his leg.

He looked towards his fallen foe. The beast which Hew Argech had ridden had picked up the man in its mouth and was dragging him away.

It suddenly occurred to Corum that the beast rather than the rider was the true master. He could not explain why he felt this, save that for a second he had looked into the beast's eyes and seen what looked like irony there.

And as he was dragged, Hew Argech opened his mouth to call to Corum in that same ingenuous tone:

'The Fhoi Myore march,' he said. 'They know that the folk of Caer Mahlod called you. They march to destroy Caer Mahlod before you return with the spear which slew me. Farewell, Corum of the Silver Hand. I go back now to my brothers, the pines.'

And soon beast and man had disappeared beyond a hill and Corum was alone, holding the spear which had saved his life, turning it this way and that in the grey light as if he thought that by inspecting it he would understand how it had come to return to his hand after it had aided him.

Then he shook his head, dismissed the mystery, and urged his horse to gallop faster through the clinging snow, still heading for Caer Mahlod. Heading there with even greater urgency than he had had before.

The Fhoi Myore were still an enigma. Every description of them he had heard had somehow not explained how they could command creatures like Hew Argech, how they could work such strange enchantments, control the Hounds of Kerenos and their Ghoolegh huntsmen. Some saw the Fhoi Myore as insensate creatures, little more than beasts; others saw them as gods. They must have some kind of intelligence, surely, if they could create the likes of Hew Argech, brother of the trees?

At first he had wondered if the Fhoi Myore were related to the Chaos Lords whom he had fought so long in past times. But the Fhoi Myore were at once less man-like and more man-like than the Chaos Lords had been, and their aims seemed different. They had had no choice, it seemed, in coming to this plane. They had fallen through a gap in the fabric of the multiverse and had been unable to return to their own strange half-world between the planes. Now they sought to recreate Limbo on Earth. Corum found that he could feel a certain sympathy for their plight, even.

He wondered if Goffanon's prediction had been a true one, or whether the prediction had been the product of Goffanon's own sense of despair. Was the doom of the Mabden inevitable?

Looking across the bleak, snow-covered land, it was easy to believe that it was their fate – and his – to die, victims of the Fhoi Myore encroachment.

He camped less frequently now, sometimes riding wildly through the night, careless of the pitfalls, half-asleep in his saddle. And his war-horse galloped less readily through the snow.

Once, in the evening, he saw a line of figures in the distance. Mist swirled around the figures as they marched or rode in huge chariots. He almost hailed them before he realised that they were not Mabden. Were these the Fhoi Myore on the march to Caer Mahlod?

And several times during his ride he heard a distant howling and he guessed that the hunting packs, the Hounds of Kerenos, were seeking him. Doubtless Hew Argech had returned to his masters and told them of how he had fallen before the spear Bryionak, which had then wrenched itself from his body and settled back in Corum's silver hand.

Caer Mahlod still seemed very distant and the cold seemed to eat into Corum's body like a worm which fed on his very blood.

More snow had fallen since he had first ridden this way and the snow had succeeded in disguising many landmarks. This fact, coupled with his blurring eyesight, made it difficult for him to find his way at all. He prayed that the horse knew the route back to Caer Mahlod and he came to trust more and more in the beast's instincts.

As exhaustion overwhelmed him he began to know a deep despair. Why had he not listened to Goffanon and lived out his days in the tranquillity of Hy-Breasail? What did he owe to these Mabden? Had he not fought enough in Mabden battles? What had that folk ever given him?

And then he would remember. They had given him Rhalina.

And he remembered Medhbh, too, King Mannach's daughter. Red-haired Medhbh in her war-gear, with her sling and her tathlum, waiting for him to bring salvation back to Caer Mahlod.

They had given him hatred, the Mabden, when they slew his family, cut off his hand and tore out his eye. They had given him fear, terror and a thirst for vengeance.

But they had also given him love. They had given him Rhalina. Now they gave him Medhbh.

These thoughts would sustain him a little, even warm him a little, drive the despair to the edges of his mind, and he would ride on. Ride on for Caer Mahlod, the fortress on the hill, and those whose only hope he remained.

But Caer Mahlod seemed to grow farther away. It seemed a year since he had seen the Fhoi Myore war-chariots on the horizon, heard the howling of the hounds. Perhaps Caer Mahlod had already fallen; perhaps he would find Medhbh frozen as those others had been frozen, in battle-posture, unaware that there would be no battle for them to fight, that they had already lost.

Another morning came. Corum's horse was slow now. It staggered sometimes as it caught its foot in a hidden furrow. It breathed with difficulty. Corum would have dismounted, if he could, and walked beside the horse to relieve its load, but he had neither the will nor the energy to get down. He began to regret that he had let Calatin have his scarlet robe. That small amount of extra heat might have saved his life, it now seemed. Had Calatin known this? Was that why Calatin had asked for the coat? An act of revenge?

He heard something. He raised his aching head and peered through his bloodshot, bleary eye. Figures blocking his way. Ghoolegh. He tried to straighten himself in the saddle, fumbling for his sword.

He urged his war-horse into a gallop, feebly waving the spear Bryionak, a croaking battle-cry breaking from his frost-bitten lips.

And then the horse's forelegs buckled under and it fell to the ground, pitching Corum over its head and leaving him exposed to the swords of his enemies.

But, thought Corum, as he sank into a coma, he would not feel the pain of their blades, at least, for a sense of warmth, of oblivion, was sweeping through him.

He smiled and let the darkness come.

3. THE ICE PHANTOMS

He dreamed that he sailed a massive ship over an infinity of ice. The ship was raised on runners and had fifty sails. Whales inhabited the ice, and other strange creatures, too. Then he no longer sailed the ship, but rode in a chariot drawn by bears beneath a strange, dull sky. But the ice remained. Worlds bereft of heat. Old, dead worlds in the final stages of entropy. But everywhere was ice – harsh, gleaming ice. Ice which brought death to any who dared it. Ice which was the symbol of ultimate death, the death of the very universe itself. Corum groaned in his sleep.

'It is the one I heard of.' The voice was soft, yet intrusive.

'Llaw Ereint?' came another's voice.

'Aye. Who else could it be? There is the silver hand. And that is a Sidhi face, I'd swear, though I've never seen one.'

Corum opened his single eye and glared at the speaker.

'I am dead,' said Corum, 'and would be grateful if you would allow me to be dead in peace.'

'You live,' said the youth practically. He was a boy of about sixteen. Though his face and body were thin, starved, his eyes were bright and intelligent and, like most of the Mabden Corum had found here, he was well-formed. He had a great mop of blond hair, kept back from his eyes by a simple leather band. He had a fur cape over his shoulders and the familiar gold and silver collar and bangles on arms and ankles. 'I am Bran. This is my brother, Teyrnon. You are Cremm, the god.'

'God?' Corum began to realise that the people he had seen ahead of him had been Mabden, not Fhoi Myore. He smiled at the youth. 'Do gods fall so easily from exhaustion?'

Bran shrugged and ran his fingers through his hair. 'I know nothing of the customs of gods. Could you not have been in disguise? Pretending to be a mortal in order to test us?'

'That is a fine way of looking at a rather more ordinary fact,' said Corum. He turned to look at Teyrnon and then looked in surprise at Bran again. The two were virtually identical in features, though Bran's fur cloak was from a brown bear and Teyrnon's was from a tawny wolf. Corum looked up and realised that he saw the folds of a small tent in which he lay while Bran and Teyrnon crouched beside him.

'Who are you?' Corum asked. 'Where are you from? Do you know aught of the fate of Caer Mahlod?'

'We are the Tuha-na-Ana – or what is left of that folk,' the youth replied. 'We are from a land to the east of Gwyddneu Garanhir, which in turn lies due south of Cremm Croich, your land. When the Fhoi Myore began to come, some of us fought them and thus perished. The rest of us – youths and old people for the most part – set off for Caer Mahlod where we heard warriors resisted the Fhoi Myore. We lost our way and had to hide many times from the Fhoi Myore and their dogs, but now we are only a short distance from Caer Mahlod, which lies west of here.'

'Caer Mahlod is my destination, too,' said Corum, sitting up. 'I carry the spear Bryionak with me and would tame the Bull of Crinanass.'

'That Bull cannot be tamed,' said Teyrnon softly. 'We saw it less than two weeks since. We were hungry and hunted it for its meat, but it turned on our hunters and slew five of them with its sharp horns before it went away towards the west.'

'If the Bull cannot be tamed,' said Corum, accepting the

mug of thin soup which Bran handed him and sipping it gratefully, 'then Caer Mahlod is lost and you would be wiser to seek some other sanctuary.'

'We were looking for Hy-Breasail,' Bran told him seriously. 'The Enchanted Isle beyond the sea. We thought we might be happy there and safe from the Fhoi Myore.'

'Safe from the Fhoi Myore you would be,' Corum said, 'but not from your own fears. Do not seek Hy-Breasail, Bran of the Tuha-na-Ana, for it means awful death to Mabden folk. No, we shall all go together to Caer Mahlod, if the Fhoi Myore do not find us first, and I will see if I can speak to the Bull of Crinanass and make him see our point of view.'

Bran shook his head sceptically. Teyrnon, his twin, echoed the gesture.

'We move on again in a few minutes,' Teyrnon told Corum. 'Will you be fit to ride again, then?'

'Is my horse still alive?'

'Alive and rested. We found a little grass for him.'

'Then I am fit to ride,' said Corum.

There were less than thirty people in the band which moved slowly across the snow, and of those thirty more than a score were old men and women. There were three other boys like Bran and his brother Teyrnon, and there were three girls, one of whom was less than ten years old. The younger children, it was learned, had perished in a sudden raid which the Hounds of Kerenos had made on the camp when the remnants of the tribe had first begun its trek to Caer Mahlod. Snow rimed the hair of all and made it sparkle. Corum joked that they were all kings and queens and wearing diamond crowns. They had been weaponless before he came and now he distributed his gear among them – a sword to one, a dirk to another, a lance each to two more, and his bow and arrows to Bran. He kept only the spear Bryionak as he rode at the head of the column, or walked beside his horse which would take two or three old people at a time, for few had eaten much in recent months and they were all light enough.

Bran had estimated that they were still two days from Caer Mahlod, but the going began to get easier, the farther west they travelled. Corum's spirits had begun to rise considerably and his horse's energy was increasing so that he was able to make short gallops ahead to spy out the land. Judging by the improvement in the weather, the Fhoi Myore had not yet reached the hill fortress.

The little party entered a valley late on the afternoon of what they hoped would be their last full day of travelling. It was not a particularly deep valley but it offered some shelter from the icy wind which occasionally blew across the moor, and they welcomed any shelter. Corum noticed that on the slopes of the hills on either side of them were gleaming formations of ice which had perhaps been formed from waterfalls blown by a wind coming from the east. They were some distance into the valley and had decided to make camp for the night, although the sun had not yet set, when Corum looked up from watching the youths erecting the tents and saw a movement. He had been sure that one of the ice-shapes had changed its position. He put this down to his own tired vision and the failing light.

And then more of the shapes were moving and it was unmistakable – they converged on the camp.

Corum shouted the alarm and began to run towards his horse. The shapes were like gleaming phantoms, darting down the slopes into the valley. Corum saw an old woman at the far end of the camp throw up her arms in horror and turn to escape, but a shimmering, ghostly figure seemed to absorb her and drag her back up the hill. Before hardly anyone was aware of it, two more old women were seized and dragged away.

Now the camp was in a furore. Bran shot two accurate shafts at the ice phantoms, but the arrows merely passed through them. Corum hurled the spear Bryionak at another and took it where its head might be, but Bryionak came sailing back to his hand without having harmed the phantom. However, it seemed that the things were timid for, once they had taken their prey, they faded back again into the hills. Corum heard Bran

127

and Teyrnon shout and begin to run together up the steep slopes in pursuit of one of the phantoms. Corum called to them that the chase would be futile and would put them in even greater danger, but they would not listen. Corum paused for a moment and then followed.

The darkness was creeping in now. Shadows fell across the snow. The sky bore only a tinge of sunlight, a smear of blood in milk. At the best of times this was poor light for hunting – and the ice phantoms would be hard to see in the full brightness of noon.

Corum managed to keep Bran and Teyrnon in sight, but only just. Bran had paused to shoot a third arrow at what he thought to be an ice phantom. Teyrnon pointed and they ran off in another direction altogether, Corum still calling to them, though he feared to attract the attention of the strange creatures the two boys pursued.

It grew darker still.

'Bran!' shouted Corum. 'Teyrnon!'

And then he found them and they were kneeling in the snow and they were weeping. Corum looked and saw that they knelt beside what was probably the body of one of the old women.

'Is she dead?' he murmured.

'Aye,' said Bran, 'our mother is dead.'

Corum had not known that one of the women had been the youths' mother. He let out a deep, long sigh and turned away, and looked into the shadowy, grinning faces of three of the phantoms.

Corum cried out, raising Bryionak to stab at the things. Silently the phantoms moved upon him. He felt their tendrils touch his skin and his flesh began to freeze. This was how they paralysed their victim and this was how they fed, drawing his heat into their own bodies. Perhaps this was how those people he had seen before had died, beside the lake. Corum despaired of saving either his life or those of the two boys. There was no means of fighting such intangible foes.

And then the tip of the spear Bryionak began to glow a peculiar orange-red, and when the tip touched one of the ice phantoms the creature hissed and disappeared, becoming no more than a cloud of steam in the air; and then the steam dispersed. Corum did not question the power of the spear. He swung it at the other two phantoms, touching them lightly with the glowing tip, and they, too, vanished. It was as if the ice phantoms needed heat to live, but too much heat overloaded them and they perished.

'We must make fires,' Corum told the boys. 'Brands. That will keep them away. And we will not camp here. We will march – by torchlight. It does not matter if the Fhoi Myore or any of their servants see us. It would be best to reach Caer Mahlod as soon as possible, for we have no means of knowing what other creatures like these the Fhoi Myore command.'

Bran and Teyrnon picked up their mother's corpse between them and began to follow Corum down the hillside. The tip of the spear Bryionak now faded again until it looked as it had always looked – merely a well-made spearhead.

In the camp Corum told the others of his decision and all were agreed.

And so they moved on, the ice phantoms lurking just beyond the light which the torches cast, making small gasping sounds, little wet sounds, pleading sounds until they had passed through the valley and were on the other side.

The phantoms did not follow them, but still they marched on, for the wind had turned for the moment and it brought the salty smell of the sea and they knew that they must surely be close to Caer Mahlod and sanctuary. But they knew, too, that the Fhoi Myore and all whom the Fhoi Myore commanded were nearby, and this gave even the oldest of the folk new energy and speed and all prayed that they would be spared until the morning when they must surely see Caer Mahlod ahead.

4. THE COLD FOLK'S MASSING

The Conical Hill was there and the stone walls of the fortress were there and King Mannach's sea-beast banner was there and there was Medhbh, beautiful Medhbh, riding a horse from the gates of Caer Mahlod and waving to him and laughing, her red hair flying and her green-grey eyes all alight with joy, her horse's hooves sending up a flurry of frost as she cried out to him:

'Corum! Corum! Corum Llaw Ereint, do you bring the spear Bryionak?'

'Aye,' Corum called back, brandishing the spear, 'and I bring guests to Caer Mahlod. We are hasty, for the Fhoi Myore are not far behind.'

She reached his side and leaned over to fling an arm about his neck and kiss him full upon the lips so that all his earlier gloom left him suddenly and he was glad that he had not stayed in Hy-Breasail, that he had not been killed by Hew Argech, that he had not been drained of his body's heat by the ice phantoms.

'You are here, Corum,' she said.

'I am here, lovely Medhbh. And here is the spear Bryionak.'

She looked at it in wonder, but she would not touch it,

even when he offered it to her. She drew back. She smiled strangely. 'It is not for me to hold. That is the spear Bryionak. That is the spear of Cremm Croich, of Llaw Ereint, of the Sidhi, of the gods and the demigods of our race. That is the spear Bryionak.'

He laughed at the serious expression which had come suddenly upon her face and he kissed her so that her eyes cleared and she laughed back at him and then turned her chestnut mare to gallop ahead of the weary band, to lead the way through the narrow gate into the fortress town of Caer Mahlod.

And there, on the other side of the gate's passage, stood King Mannach, smiling in gratitude and respect at Corum, who had found one of the great treasures of Caer Llud, one of the lost treasures of the Mabden, the spear which could tame the last member of a herd of Sidhi cattle, the Black Bull of Crinanass.

'Greetings, Lord of the Mound,' said King Mannach without pomposity. 'Greetings, hero. Greetings, son.'

Corum swung down from the saddle, and again he stretched out the silver hand which held Bryionak. 'Here it is. Look at it. It is an ordinary spear, King Mannach – or seems so. Yet it has already saved my life twice upon my journey back to Caer Mahlod. Inspect it, and tell me if you think it an unusual spear.'

But King Mannach followed the example of his daughter and backed away from the spear. 'No, Prince Corum, only a hero may carry the spear Bryionak, for a lesser mortal would be cursed if he tried to hold it. It is a Sidhi weapon. Even when it was in our possession it was kept in a case and the spear itself was never touched.'

'Well,' said Corum, 'I'll respect your customs, though there is nothing at all to fear from the spear. Only our enemies should fear Bryionak.'

'As you say,' said King Mannach in a subdued tone. Then he smiled. 'Now we must eat. We caught fish today and there are several hares. Let all these people come with us to the hall and eat, too, for they look hungry indeed.'

Bran and Teyrnon spoke for their few surviving clansfolk.

'We accept your hospitality, great king, for we are fair famished. And we offer you our services, as warriors, to aid you in your fight against the fierce Fhoi Myore.'

King Mannach inclined his noble head. 'My hospitality is poor compared with your pride and your pledge and I thank you, warrior, for your presence at our battlements.'

As King Mannach spoke the last word there came a shout from above and a girl who had been on guard above the gate called:

'White mist boiling on the north and south. The Cold Folk are massing. The Fhoi Myore come.'

King Mannach said, not without humour, 'I fear that the banquet will have to be postponed. Let us hope it will be a victory feast.' He smiled grimly. 'And that the fish is still fresh when we've finished our fight!'

King Mannach turned to Corum after directing more of his men to the walls. 'You must call the Bull of Crinanass, Corum. You must call it soon. If it does not come then we are over, the folk of Caer Mahlod.'

'I do not know how to call the Bull, King Mannach.'

'Medhbh knows. She will teach you.'

'I know,' said Medhbh.

Then she and Corum joined the warriors on the walls and looked eastward; and there were the Fhoi Myore with their mist and their minions.

'They do not come for sport this day,' said Medhbh.

With his right hand Corum took her left hand, holding it tightly.

About two miles distant, beyond the forest, they saw pale mist churning. It covered the whole horizon from north to south and it moved slowly but purposefully towards Caer Mahlod. Ahead of this mist were many packs of hounds, questing and scenting as ordinary dogs run ahead of a hunt. Behind the hounds were small figures whom Corum guessed were white-faced Ghoolegh huntsmen and behind these huntsmen were riders, pale green riders who, like Hew Argech, were doubtless brothers to the pines. But in the mist itself could be detected larger shapes, the shapes Corum had seen only once before. These were the dark outlines of monstrous war-chariots drawn by beasts which were certainly not horses. And there were seven of these chariots and in the chariots were seven riders of enormous size.

'A great massing,' said Medhbh, in a voice which succeeded in sounding brave. 'They send their whole strength against us. All seven of the Fhoi Myore come. They must respect us greatly, those gods.'

'We shall give them cause,' said Corum.

'Now we must leave Caer Mahlod,' Medhbh told him.

'Desert the city?'

'We have to go to call the Bull of Crinanass. There is a place. The only place to which the Bull will come.'

Corum was reluctant to go. 'In a few hours – perhaps in less time than that – the Fhoi Myore will attack.'

'We must try to return by that time. That is why it is urgent that we go now to the Sidhi Rock and seek the Bull.'

So they left Caer Mahlod quietly, on fresh horses, and rode along the cliffs above a sea which groaned and roared and rolled as if in anticipation of the coming struggle.

At last they stood upon yellow sand with the dark and jagged cliffs behind them and the uneasy sea before them and looked up at a strange rock which stood alone on the beach. It had begun to rain and the rain and the sea-spray lashed the rock and made it shine with a peculiar variety of soft colours which veined it. And in places the rock was opaque and in other places it was almost completely transparent so that other, warmer colours could be seen at its heart.

'The Sidhi Rock,' said Medhbh.

Corum nodded. What else could the rock be? It was not of this plane. Perhaps, like the island of Hy-Breasail, it had come with the Sidhi when they journeyed here to fight the Cold Folk. He has seen things like it before – objects which had no real place upon this plane, which had part of themselves in another plane altogether.

The wind blew the water against his face. It blew their hair and their cloaks about them and they had difficulty climbing the smooth, worn stone and standing at last on the top of the rock. Huge waves rolled down upon the coast. Great gusts threatened to blow them from their perch. Rain washed down them and cascaded over the rock so that small waterfalls were formed.

'Now take the spear Bryionak in your silver hand,' directed Medhbh. 'Raise it high.'

Corum obeyed her.

'Now you must translate what I tell you into your speech, the pure Vadhagh tongue, for that is the same tongue as the Sidhi.'

'I know,' said Corum. 'What must I say?'

'Before you speak you must think of the bull, the Black Bull of Crinanass. He is as tall at the shoulder as you are at the head. He has a long coat of black hair. His horns are wider from tip to tip than you can stretch your arms, and they are sharp, those horns. Can you picture such a creature?'

'I think so.'

'Then speak this and speak it clearly:'

All around them the day was turning grey, save for the great rock on which they stood.

You shall pass through tall gates of stone, you, Black Bull.
You shall come forth from where you dwell when Cremm Croich calls.
If you sleep, Black Bull, awaken now.
If you wake, Black Bull, then rise now.
If you rise, Black Bull, then walk. Shake the earth, Black Bull.
Come to the rock where you were sired, where you were born, Black Bull.
For he who holds the spear is master of your fate.
Bryionak, forged at Crinanass and mined from Sidhi stone,
Fights once more the dread Fhoi Myore, whom you must fight, Black Bull.
Come, Black Bull. Come, Black Bull. Come home.'

Medhbh had spoken this whole thing without drawing breath. Now her grey-green eyes looked anxiously into his single eye. 'Can you translate that into your own speech?'

'Aye,' said Corum. 'But why would a beast come to answer such chanting?'

'Do not question that, Corum.'

The Vadhagh shrugged.

'Do you still see the Bull in your mind's eye?'

He paused. Then he nodded. 'I do.'

'Then I will speak the lines again and you will repeat them in the Vadhagh tongue.'

And Corum obeyed, though the chant seemed a crude one to him and hardly Vadhagh in origin. Slowly he repeated what she told him and, as he chanted, he began to feel light-headed. The words began to trip from his lips. He declaimed them. He stood at his full height, clothing and hair blown this way and that by the grey wind, and he held the spear Bryionak high, and he called for the Bull of Crinanass. His voice grew louder and louder and sounded above the wind's snore.

'Come, Black Bull! Come, Black Bull! Come home!'

Speaking the words in his own tongue somehow seemed to give them more weight, though the language Medhbh spoke was scarcely different from the Vadhagh language.

When the words were finished, she put a hand on his arm and a finger to her lips and they listened through the howling wind and the crashing sea and the cascading rain and heard a distant lowing from somewhere, and the Sidhi rock seemed to glow with richer colours and tremble a little.

The lowing came again, closer.

Medhbh was grinning at him, holding his arm very tightly now.

'The Bull,' she whispered. 'The Bull comes.'

But still they could not tell from which direction the lowing reached their ears.

The rain fell in even heavier sheets until they could barely see beyond the rock at all and it was as if the sea had engulfed them.

But the sounds began to merge into one sound and that sound gradually became identified as the deep, reflective lowing of a bull. They peered from where they stood on the top of the Sidhi Rock and it seemed to them that they saw the great Bull bring its great, black bulk up out of the waters of the sea and stand shaking itself upon the shore, turning its huge, intelligent eyes from side to side as it sought the source of the chant which had brought it here.

'Black Bull!' cried Medhbh. 'Black Bull of Crinanass! Here stands Cremm Croich and the spear Bryionak. Here stands your destiny!'

And the monstrous Bull lowered its head with the sharp, wide-spaced horns, and it shook its shaggy black body, and it pawed at the sand with its heavy hooves. And they could smell its warm body; they could smell the comforting, familiar stink of cattle. But this was like no familiar farmyard beast. This was a war-beast, proud and confident, a beast which served not a master but an ideal.

It swung its black tufted tail from side to side as it stared up at the two people who stood side by side on the Sidhi Rock and who stared back at it in wonder.

'Now I know why the Fhoi Myore fear that beast,' said Corum.

5. THE
BLOOD-HARVESTING

As Corum and Medhbh descended somewhat nervously from the Sidhi Rock, the Bull's eyes remained fixed on the spear which Corum carried. Now the animal stood very still, looming over them as they approached it, its head still slightly lowered. It seemed as suspicious of them as they were fearful of it, yet it was plain that it recognised Bryionak, and that it had respect for that spear.

'Bull,' said Corum, and he did not feel foolish for speaking to a beast in this way, 'will you come with us to Caer Mahlod?'

The rain had turned to sleet now and the sleet glistened on the Bull's black flanks. Farther along the beach the horses were showing signs of fear. They were more than suspicious of the Black Bull of Crinanass: they were in stark terror of it. But the Bull ignored the horses. It shook its head, and droplets of moisture flew from the tips of its two sharp horns. Its nostrils quivered. Its hard, intelligent eyes glanced once at the horses and then returned to gaze upon the spear.

Although Corum had, in the past, been in the presence of much larger creatures, he had never confronted an animal which gave such a strong impression of power. It seemed to him at that moment that nothing on Earth could stand against the massive Bull.

Corum and Medhbh left the Bull watching them and crossed the wind-blown sand to calm their horses. They succeeded eventually in soothing them enough so that they could be ridden, but they were still skittish. Then, for there was naught else they could do, they began to ride up the cliff-paths, going back towards Caer Mahlod.

After a few minutes, when it remained stock still, as if considering a problem, the Black Bull of Crinanass started to follow them, its hooves moving surely along the narrow path, though it never came very close to them. Perhaps, thought Corum, such a beast as that disdained to keep intimate company with mortals as weak as themselves.

And the sleet soon turned to snow and the snow blew cold and fierce upon the cliffs of the west, and Corum and Medhbh knew that these were signs that the Fhoi Myore approached and might, even now, have reached the walls of Caer Mahlod.

It was indeed a horrid massing which had collected at the walls of the Mabden fortress as scum might collect around a proud ship's hull. The white mist was thick, almost viscous, but it still clung largely to the forest and usually in parts of the forest where there were conifers. Here hid the Fhoi Myore themselves, and the mist was necessary to them – it was a limbo-mist which sustained them; without it they would be ill at ease. Corum saw the seven dark shapes moving about in it. They had left their chariots and seemed to be conferring. Kerenos himself, Chief of the Fhoi Myore, must be there. And Balahr who, like Corum, had but one eye, but a deadly eye. And Goim, the female Fhoi Myore, with a taste for the manhood of mortals. And the others.

Corum and Medhbh reined in their horses and turned to see if the Black Bull still followed.

It did. It stopped when they stopped, its eyes still upon the spear Bryionak.

The fight had begun. The Hounds of Kerenos leapt at the

walls as they had leapt before. But the Ghoolegh ran against the Mabden, too, with bows and spears. And the pale green riders charged the gate, led by one who was unmistakably Hew Argech, whom Corum should have slain. Even from where they watched upon an eminence looking down upon Caer Mahlod, Corum and Medhbh could hear the cries of the defenders and the howlings of the dreadful dogs.

'How can we reach our folk now?' Medhbh said in despair.

'Even if we reached the gates they would be fools to open them to admit us,' Corum agreed. 'We must confine ourselves, I suppose, to attacking them from the rear until they realise that we are behind them.'

Medhbh nodded. She pointed. 'Let us ride over there, where the walls are almost breached. We might be able to give our folk time to repair the damage.'

Corum saw that her suggestion had sense in it. Without a word he spurred his horse down the hill, the spear Bryionak poised for a cast at the first of his foes that he should meet. He was almost certain that he and Medhbh would die, but at that moment he did not care. All he regretted was that he would not die in his name-robe, the scarlet robe he had given to Calatin on the coast of Moidel's Mount.

As he rode nearer, he was able to see that the ice-phantoms were not in this army. Perhaps those creatures were not the creations of the Fhoi Myore, after all? But the Ghoolegh were, that was certain. Being almost indestructible they were proving a hard enemy for the Mabden to cope with. And who led them into battle? A rider on a tall horse. A rider who was not pale green, like Hew Argech, yet still familiar. How many men were familiar to him in this world? Very few. The light caught the armour of the rider. In a moment it had changed from bright gold to dull silver, from scarlet to flickering blue.

And Corum knew he had seen that armour before and that he, himself, had sent its wearer to Limbo in a great fight at the camp of Queen Xiombarg's forces. To Limbo – where the Fhoi Myore, perhaps, were still secure, before the disruption of the fabric of the multiverse had sent them into this world to poison it. And had it sent that rider with them? It was a likely explanation. The dark yellow plume still nodded on the rider's helm which, as before, completely obscured the face. The breastplate was still engraved with the Arms of Chaos, the eight arrows radiating from a central hub. And in his glove of metal was a sword which also shone sometimes gold, sometimes silver, sometimes blue or scarlet.

'Gaynor,' said Corum, and he recalled the terror of Gaynor's death. 'It is Prince Gaynor the Damned.'

'You know that warrior?' she said.

'I slew him once,' said Corum grimly. 'Or, at least, I banished him – I thought from this world, at least. But there he is. My old enemy. Could he be the "brother", I wonder, of whom the old woman spoke?' This last question was addressed to himself. He had already drawn back his arm and flung Bryionak towards Prince Gaynor, who had once been a champion (perhaps the Champion Eternal himself) but was now pledged wholly to evil.

Bryionak went flying to its target and it struck Prince Gaynor's shoulder and made him stagger in his saddle. The faceless helm turned and watched as the spear flew back to Corum's hand. Gaynor had been directing his Ghoolegh against the weak parts of Caer Mahlod's walls. They ran through the snow which had been stained red by blood and black by mud; many were missing limbs, features and even innards, but still they worked. Corum gripped the spear Bryionak, and he knew that, as before, Gaynor was not easily beaten, even by magic.

He heard Gaynor's laughter from within the helm. Gaynor seemed almost pleased to see him, as if glad to see a familiar face whether it was friend's or foe's. 'Prince Corum, the Champion of the Mabden! We were speculating on your absence, thinking that you had sensibly fled, perhaps even returning to your own world. But here you are. How whimsical is Fate that she wills us to continue our silly squabble.'

Corum looked back for a moment and saw that the Bull of Crinanass still followed. He looked beyond Gaynor at the battered walls of Caer Mahlod. He saw many dead men on the battlements.

'Indeed she is,' he said. 'But would you fight me again, Prince Gaynor? Would you beg me for mercy again? Would you have me send you to Limbo again?'

Prince Gaynor laughed his bitter laugh and said:

'Ask the Fhoi Myore that last question. They would be only too pleased to return to their dreadful homeland. And if they left me and if I had no loyalties, now that Chaos and Law no longer war upon this plane, I should be pleased to join with you, Corum. As it is, as usual, we must battle.'

Corum remembered what he had seen on Gaynor's face the time he had opened the man's helm. He shuddered. Again he felt pity for Gaynor the Damned who was bound to live out many existences in many different planes, just as was Corum — though Gaynor was destined to serve the meanest, the most treacherous of masters. And now his soldiers were half-dead things. Previously they had been beast-things.

'The quality of your infantry seems up to standard,' said Corum.

Gaynor laughed again, his voice muffled from within his never-opened helm. 'Even better, in some respects, I'd say.'

'Would you not call them off and join with me, Gaynor? You know that I had little hatred for you at the end. We have more in common than any others here.'

'True,' said Gaynor. 'So why not side with me, Corum? After all, Fhoi Myore conquest is inevitable.'

'And will inevitably lead to death.'

'That is what I have been promised,' said Gaynor simply.

And Corum knew that Gaynor wanted death more than anything and that he could not argue with the damned Prince unless he, Corum, could offer Gaynor a death that was still quicker.

'When the world dies,' Gaynor continued, 'shall not I die, too?'

Corum looked beyond Prince Gaynor the Damned, at the battlements of Caer Mahlod and the handful of Mabden fighting for their lives against half-dead Ghoolegh, snapping devil dogs and creatures who were more trees than men. 'It is possible, Gaynor,' he said thoughtfully, 'that it is your doom to be forever siding with evil in an effort to gain your ends, when if you achieved a noble deed your wishes would be granted.'

'A romantic view, I fear, Prince Corum.' Gaynor turned his horse away.

'What ?' said Corum. 'You will not fight me ?'

'Nay – nor your bovine friend,' said Gaynor. He rode back towards the cover of the mist. 'I wish to remain on this world until the finish. I'll not be sent back to Limbo again by you!' His tone was equable, even friendly, as he cried: 'But I'll return later to look upon your corpse, Corum.'

'You think it will be here ?'

'We think that perhaps thirty of your folk are left alive and that before the evening our hounds will be feasting within your walls. Therefore – yes, I think your corpse will be here. Farewell, Corum.'

And Gaynor had gone; and Corum and Medhbh were riding on for the broken wall and now they heard the Black Bull of Crinanass snorting behind them. They thought at first it chased them for daring to summon it, but it veered off and charged at a knot of pale green riders who had sighted Corum and Medhbh and had intended to ride them down.

The Black Bull of Crinanass lowered its head and drove straight into the group of riders, scattering their beasts, tossing men high into the air and then charging onward, straight into a rank of Ghoolegh, trampling every one of them, turning, its tail high and its head nodding, to spike a devil dog on each horn.

It dominated the whole battlefield, that Black Bull of Crinanass. It shook off any weapons which might find a mark in its hide. It charged with fearful speed thrice around the walls of Caer Mahlod while Corum and Medhbh, forgotten by their enemies, looked on with stunned delight. And Corum held the spear Bryionak high into the air, and cheered the Black Bull of Crinanass until he saw that there was a gap in the ranks of the stunned besiegers and he lowered his head, bade Medhbh to follow him, and urged his horse towards Caer Mahlod, leaping it through the breach and stopping it, by chance, directly before a weary and much-wounded King Mannach who sat upon a rock trying to stop the blood flowing from his mouth while an old man tried to remove the arrow-head from his lung.

There were tears in King Mannach's eyes as he lifted his old, noble head to stare at Corum. 'But the Bull has come too late,' he said.

'Too late, perhaps,' said Corum, 'but at least you will see the Bull destroy those who have destroyed your folk.'

'No,' said King Mannach. 'I will not watch. I am tired of it.'

As Medhbh comforted her father, Corum went around the walls of Caer Mahlod, taking stock of their situation while the Bull of Crinanass occupied the enemy outside.

Prince Gaynor had been wrong. There were not thirty able-bodied men left on the walls, but forty. And outside were still many of the hounds, several squadrons of pale green riders and a fair number of Ghoolegh. Moreover the Fhoi Myore themselves had yet to move upon Caer Mahlod and any one of the gods of Limbo probably had the power to destroy the city if he cared to leave his misty sanctuary for a few moments.

Corum climbed to the highest tower of the battlements, now partially in ruins. The Bull was chasing little groups of their enemies all over the muddy battlefield. Many were fleeing, heedless of the chilling, booming noises which came from the mist over the forest – the voices, no doubt, of the Fhoi Myore. And those who did not heed the voices were as doomed as those who paused, turned and were destroyed by the mighty Bull, for they did not run far before they fell dead, slain by their own masters.

The Fhoi Myore did not seem to care that they wasted their creatures so and yet did nothing to stop the carnage which the Black Bull of Crinanass was wreaking. Corum supposed that the Cold Folk knew that they could still crush Caer Mahlod and perhaps deal with the Bull, too.

And then it was over. Not a single Ghoolegh, not a single hound and not a single pale green rider remained alive. What mortal weapons could not slay, the Black Bull had slain.

It stood triumphant amongst the corpses of men, beasts and things that were like men. It pawed at the ground and its breath foamed from its nostrils. It raised its head and it bellowed and that bellow shook the walls of Caer Mahlod.

Yet still the Fhoi Myore had not moved from their mist.

None on the battlements cheered, for they knew that the main attack was still to come.

Now, save for the great Bull's triumphant lowing, there was a silence about the scene. Death was everywhere. Death hung over the battlefield; Death inhabited the fortress. And Death waited in the mist-shrouded forest. Corum remembered something King Mannach had told him – how the Fhoi Myore pursued Death. Did they, like Prince Gaynor, long for oblivion? Was this their main concern? If so, it made them an even more terrifying enemy.

The mist had begun to move. Corum cried out to the survivors to ready themselves. In his silver hand he held up the spear Bryionak, so that all could see.

'Here is the spear of the Sidhi! There is the last of the Sidhi war-cattle! And here stands Corum Llaw Ereint. Rally, men of Caer Mahlod, for the Fhoi Myore come against us now in all their strength. But we have strength. We have courage. And this is our land, our world, and we must defend it!'

Corum saw Medhbh. He saw her smile up at him and heard her cry out:

'If we die then let us die in a way that will make our legend great!'

Even King Mannach, leaning on the arm of a warrior who was, himself, wounded, seemed to recover from his depression. Sound men and wounded men, youths and maidens, the aged, now swarmed up to the walls of Caer Mahlod and steadied their hearts as they saw seven shadows in seven creaking battle-carts drawn by seven misshapen beasts reach the bottom of the hill upon which Caer Mahlod stood. And the mist surrounded them again, and the Black Bull of Crinanass was also engulfed in the pale, clinging stuff, and they no longer heard his lowing. It was as if the mist had poisoned him and perhaps that was what had happened.

Corum took aim at the first looming shadow, aiming for what appeared to be the head, though the outline was much distorted. The creaking of the chariots grated on his bones and his body wanted to do little but curl in on itself, but he resisted the sensation and cast the spear Bryionak.

Slowly the spear seemed to sunder the mist as it passed through and went true to its target and produced, for an instant, a strange honk of pain. Then the spear returned to his hand and the honking continued. In other circumstances the sound might have been ludicrous, but here it was sinister and menacing. It was the voice of an insensate beast, of a stupid being, and Corum realised that the owner of that voice was a creature of little intelligence and monstrous will, of primitive will. That was what made the Fhoi Myore so dangerous. They were motivated by blind need, they could not understand their plight, they could think of no way to deal with it but to continue their conquests, continue them without malice, or hatred or any sense of vengeance. They used what they needed, they made use of whatever powers they had, of whoever would serve them, to seek an impossible goal. Yes, that was what made them almost impossible to defeat. They could not be bargained with, reasoned with. Fear was all that might stop them and it was plain that the one who had honked did fear the Sidhi spear. The advancing chariots began to slow as the Fhoi Myore grunted to each other.

A moment later a face appeared out of the mist. It was more like a wound than a face. It was red and there were lumps of raw flesh hanging on it and the mouth was distorted and appeared in the left cheek and there was but one eye – one eye with a great lid of dead flesh. And attached to that eye-lid was a wire which ran over the skull and under the arm-pit and could be pulled by the two-fingered hand to open the eye-lid.

The hand moved now, tugging at the wire. Corum was filled with an instinctive feeling of danger and was already ducking behind the battlement as the eye opened. The eye was blue, like northern ice, and from it poured a radiance. Bitter cold gnawed at Corum's body, though he was not in the direct path of that radiance. And now he knew how those people by the lake had died, frozen in the postures of war. The cold was so intense that it knocked him backward and almost off the ledge. He recovered, crawled farther away and raised his head, the spear poised. Already several of the warriors on the battlements were rigid and dead. Corum threw the spear Bryionak. He threw it at the blue eye.

For one moment it seemed that Bryionak had been frozen in the air. It hovered, suspended, and then appeared to make a conscious effort to continue, and the point, glowing bright orange now, as it had glowed against the ice phantoms, sliced into the eye.

Then Corum knew from which of the Fhoi Myore the honking had come. The hand dropped the wire and the eye-lid closed even as the spear withdrew itself and returned to Corum. The travesty of a face twisted and the head turned this way and that, while the beast which pulled the chariot lurched round and began to retreat into the mist.

Corum felt a certain elation enter his mind. This Sidhi weapon had been especially made to fight the Fhoi Myore and it did its job well. Now one of the six was in retreat.

Corum called out to the people on the wall:

'Get back to the ground. Leave me here alone, for I have the spear Bryionak. Your weapons can do nothing against the Fhoi Myore. Let me stand here and fight them.'

Medhbh cried back: 'Let me stand with you, Corum, to die with you!'

But he shook his head and turned again to regard the advancing Cold Folk. Still it was hard to see them. A suggestion of a horned head. A hint of bristling hair. A glint which might have been the glint of an eye.

There came a roaring, then. Was that the voice of Kerenos, chieftain of the Fhoi Myore? No. The roaring came from behind the Fhoi Myore chariots.

An even larger, darker shape reared up behind them and Corum gasped as he recognised it. It was the Black Bull of Crinanass, grown huger but losing none of its mass. It lowered its horns and it plucked one of the Fhoi Myore from its chariot and it tossed the god up into the sky and caught the god on its horn and tossed the god again.

The Fhoi Myore were in panic. They wheeled their warcarts and began a sudden retreat. Corum saw Prince Gaynor, tiny and terrified, running with them. The mist moved faster than a tidal wave, back over the forest, out over the plain, and disappeared over the horizon leaving behind it a wasteland of corpses and the Black Bull of Crinanass which had shrunk to its previous size and was now grazing contentedly on a patch of grass somehow left untrampled on the battlefield. But on its horns were dark smears and there were pieces of meat scattered about nearby; and some distance to the left of the Black Bull of Crinanass was a huge chariot, much bigger than the Bull, which had overturned, its wheel still spinning. It was a crude thing, of wood and wicker-work poorly crafted.

The folk of Caer Mahlod were not jubilant, though they had been saved from destruction. They were stunned at what had happened. Very slowly they began to gather on the battlements to look at all the destruction.

Corum walked slowly down the steps, the spear Bryionak still held loosely in his silver hand. He walked through the tunnel and out of the gate of Caer Mahlod and he walked across the ruined earth to where the Bull was grazing. He did not know why he went to the Bull, and this time the creature did not move away from him but turned its huge head and stared into his eyes.

'You must slay me now,' said the Black Bull of Crinanass, 'and then my destiny will be complete.' It spoke in the pure tongue of the Vadhagh and the Sidhi. It spoke calmly, yet sadly.

'I cannot slay you,' said Corum. 'You have saved us all. You killed one of the Fhoi Myore so that now they number only six. Caer Mahlod still stands and many of her folk still live because of what you did.'

'It is what you did,' said the Bull. 'You found the spear Bryionak. You called me. I knew what must happen.'

'Why must I slay you?'

'It is my destiny. It is necessary.'

'Very well,' said Corum. 'I will do what you request.'

And he took the spear Bryionak and cast it into the heart of the Black Bull of Crinanass, and a great gout of blood burst from the Bull's side and the beast began to run, and this time the spear stayed where it was and did not return to Corum's hand.

Over the whole battlefield ran the Black Bull of Crinanass. Through the forest it ran and across the moors beyond. Along the cliffs by the sea it ran. And its blood washed the whole land, and where the blood touched the land it became green and flowers grew up and trees came into leaf. And slowly, above, the sky was clearing and the clouds fled in the wake of the Fhoi Myore and the sky became blue and the warm sun shone; and when the sun spread heat across all the world around Caer Mahlod the Bull ran towards the broken cliffs where Castle Erorn stood. And the Bull leapt the chasm which separated the cliff from the tower and it stood beside the tower for a moment, its knees buckling as the blood still trickled from its wound; it looked back at Corum, then staggered to the headland and flung itself over, into the sea. And the spear Bryionak still stayed in the side of the Black Bull of Crinanass and was never afterward seen again in mortal lands.

EPILOGUE

And that was the end of the Tale of the Bull and the Spear.

All signs of the struggle had disappeared from hill, forest and plain. Summer had come to Caer Mahlod at last and many believed that the blood of the Black Bull had made the land safe for ever from the encroachment of the Cold Folk.

And Corum Jhaelen Irsei, of the Vadhagh folk, lived a life among the Tuha-na-Cremm Croich, and that, to them, was a further guarantee of their security. Even the old woman whom Corum had met on the frozen plain no longer muttered her gloomy warnings. All were happy. And they were happy that Corum lay with Medhbh, daughter of King Mannach, for it meant that he would stay with them. They harvested their crops and they sang in the fields and they feasted well, for the land was rich again where the Bull had run.

But sometimes Corum, lying beside his new love, would awake in the night and fancy that he heard the cool and melancholy strains of a harp and he would brood on that old woman's words and would wonder why he should fear a harp, a brother and, above all, beauty.

And at those times, of all the folk dwelling at Caer Mahlod, Corum was not happy.

THIS ENDS THE FIRST VOLUME OF THE
CHRONICLE OF CORUM AND THE SILVER HAND

A SELECTION FROM THE MERCURIAL MIND OF MICHAEL MOORCOCK AVAILABLE IN MAYFLOWER BOOKS

The Cornelius Chronicles:
The Final Programme — 40p ☐

The Dancers at the End of Time:

The Hollow Lands — 75p ☐
An Alien Heat — 85p ☐
The End of All Songs — 95p ☐

Hawkmoon: The History of the Runestaff:

The Jewel in the Skull — 75p ☐
The Mad God's Amulet — 60p ☐
The Sword of the Dawn — 85p ☐
The Runestaff — 75p ☐

Hawkmoon: The Chronicles of Castle Brass:

Count Brass — 75p ☐
The Champion of Garathorm* — 60p ☐
The Quest for Tanelorn* — 60p ☐

Erekosë Series:

Eternal Champion — 85p ☐
Phoenix in Obsidian — 75p ☐
The Champion of Garathorm* — 60p ☐
The Quest for Tanelorn* — 60p ☐

Elric Series:

Stealer of Souls — 60p ☐
Stormbringer — 85p ☐
The Singing Citadel — 75p ☐

The Books of Corum:

The Knight of the Swords — 75p ☐
The Queen of the Swords — 50p ☐
The King of the Swords — 50p ☐

Other Titles:

The Winds of Limbo — 50p ☐
Behold the Man — 50p ☐
The Blood-Red Game — 60p ☐
The Black Corridor — 35p ☐
The Shores of Death — 50p ☐
The Time Dweller — 85p ☐

*interconnected series

THE WORLD'S GREATEST SCIENCE FICTION
AUTHORS NOW AVAILABLE IN PANTHER BOOKS

E E 'Doc' Smith

'Classic Lensman Series'

Masters of the Vortex	85p	☐
Children of the Lens	85p	☐
Second Stage Lensman	85p	☐
Grey Lensman	85p	☐
Galactic Patrol	75p	☐
First Lensman	85p	☐
Triplanetary	85p	☐
'Lensman' Gift Set	£4.25	☐

'Skylark Series'

The Skylark of Space	75p	
Skylark Three	75p	☐
The Skylark of Valeron	85p	☐
Skylark Duquesne	85p	☐
'Skylark' Gift Set	£3.25	☐

'Family D'Alembert Series' (with *Stephen Goldin*)

The Imperial Stars	75p	☐
Stranglers' Moon	75p	☐
The Clockwork Traitor	75p	☐
Getaway World	85p	☐
The Bloodstar Conspiracy	65p	☐
The Purity Plot	75p	☐

'Novels'

Subspace Explorers	85p	☐
Galaxy Primes	50p	☐
Spacehounds of IPC	85p	☐

THE WORLD'S GREATEST SCIENCE FICTION AUTHORS NOW AVAILABLE IN PANTHER BOOKS

Ursula K LeGuin

Orsinian Tales	75p	☐
The Wind's Twelve Quarters (*Volume 1*)	85p	☐
The Wind's Twelve Quarters (*Volume 2*)	75p	☐
The Dispossessed	95p	☐
The Left Hand of Darkness	75p	☐
The Lathe of Heaven	75p	☐
City of Illusions	75p	☐

Robert Silverberg

Earth's Other Shadow	75p	☐
A World Inside	75p	☐
Tower of Glass	60p	☐
Recalled to Life	50p	☐
A Time of Changes	50p	☐
Invaders from Earth	80p	☐
Master of Life and Death	75p	☐

All these books are available at your local bookshop or newsagent, or can be ordered direct from the publisher. Just tick the titles you want and fill in the form below.

Name..

Address ....

....

Write to Mayflower Cash Sales, PO Box 11, Falmouth, Cornwall TR10 9EN.

Please enclose remittance to the value of the cover price plus:

UK: 25p for the first book plus 10p per copy for each additional book ordered to a maximum charge of £1.05.

BFPO and EIRE: 25p for the first book plus 10p per copy for the next 8 books, thereafter 5p per book.

OVERSEAS: 40p for the first book and 12p for each additional book.

Granada Publishing reserve the right to show new retail prices on covers, which may differ from those previously advertised in the text or elsewhere.